G000255261

Joseph R_____ of the cosmopolitan, tole_____ an culture that flourished _____ ngarian Empire. Born into _____ tern edge of the empire, h_____ nd novelist. On Hitler's as_____ leave Germany and he died in poverty in Paris. Granta Books also publish his novels *Rebellion, The String of Pearls, Right and Left, The Legend of the Holy Drinker, Hotel Savoy, Job: The Story of a Simple Man, The Emperor's Tomb, The Radetzky March, Tarabas, Collected Shorter Fiction* and his non-fiction reportage books *The Wandering Jews, What I Saw: Reports From Berlin 1920–33* and its companion volume *The White Cities: Reports From France 1925–39*.

Also by Joseph Roth

NON-FICTION

The Wandering Jews
What I Saw: Reports from
Berlin 1920–33
The White Cities: Reports from
France 1925–39

FICTION

Rebellion
The String of Pearls
Right and Left
The Legend of the Holy Drinker
Hotel Savoy
Job: The Story of a Simple Man
The Emperor's Tomb
The Radetzky March
Tarabas
Weights and Measures
The Silent Prophet
The Spider's Web
Flight Without End
Zipper and His Father
Collected Shorter Fiction

THE SPIDER'S WEB

Translated from the German
by John Hoare

Joseph Roth

Granta Books
London

Granta Publications, 2/3 Hanover Yard, London N1 8BE

First published in Great Britain by Granta Books 2004

A CIP catalogue record for this book
is available from the British Library.

1 3 5 7 9 10 8 6 4 2

Printed and bound in Great Britain by
Mackays of Chatham plc

THE SPIDER'S WEB

1

Theodor grew up in the house of his father, the railway inspector of customs and former sergeant-major, Wilhelm Lohse. Little Theodor was a fair-haired, industrious and well-behaved boy. He had fervently desired the distinction he was later to achieve, but hadn't dared to expect it. One might say that he exceeded expectations which he had never had.

Father Lohse was not to see his son at his peak. The old inspector of customs was only privileged to see Theodor in the uniform of a lieutenant of the Reserve. The old man never asked for more. He died in the fourth year of the Great War, and the last moments of his life were dominated by the thought that his coffin would be followed by Lieutenant Theodor Lohse.

A year later, Theodor was no longer a lieutenant. He was reading law, and he was tutor in the household of the jeweller, Efrussi. Every day, in the jeweller's house, he was given white coffee with a skin on it and a ham sandwich on white bread, and every month he received a fee. This was the basis of his material existence, for the Technical Labour Exchange, of which he was a member, rarely provided work, and what they did provide was hard and indifferently paid. Once a week Theodor drew vegetables from the Reserve Officers' Co-operative. He shared these with his mother and sisters, in whose house he lived, tolerated rather than welcomed, scarcely noticed and, on the rare occasions when he was, rather despised. His mother was sickly, his sisters were wilting and not growing any younger. They couldn't forgive Theodor for having failed – he who had twice been mentioned in despatches – to die a hero's death as a lieutenant. A dead son would have been the pride of the family. A demobilised lieutenant, a victim of the revolution, was a burden to his womenfolk. Theodor lived amid his family like some aged grandfather who would have been revered in death but who is scorned because he is still alive.

He would have been spared much discomfort were it nor for the silent enmity which stood like a wall between him and his household. He could have told his sisters that he was not responsible for his own misfortune; that he cursed the revolution and was gnawed by hatred for the socialists and the Jews, that he bore each day like a yoke across his bowed neck and felt himself trapped in his epoch as in some sunless prison. No escape beckoned to him, and flight was impossible.

But he said nothing. He had always been a silent type, had always sensed the invisible hand before his lips, even as a boy. He could only utter what he had learned by heart, the sound of which was already prepared, formed silently a dozen times in his ears and his throat. It took him a lot of learning before the recalcitrant words would yield and take their place in his brain. He learned stories by rote, as if they were poems. The printed sentences stood before his eyes as if in a book, the page number at the top and, in the margin, a nose, doodled during some idle quarter of an hour.

Every hour bore a strange aspect. Everything surprised him. Everything which happened was frightening, because it was new, yet it vanished before making any impression. His timidity taught him to be careful, to work hard, to train himself with ruthless determination, but again and again he discovered that his preparation was insufficient. He would then work ten times as hard. Thus he had forced his way to second position in his school. First came the Jew, Glaser, who drifted smilingly through breaks, carefree and heedless of books, but who in twenty minutes could turn in an impeccable Latin exercise, and in whose head vocabularies, formulae and irregular verbs seemed to sprout effortlessly.

Young Efrussi so resembled Glaser that it was an effort for Theodor to assert his authority over the jeweller's son. Theodor had to suppress a still but obstinately growing timidity before he could correct his pupil. Young Efrussi wrote down and spoke his mistakes with such confidence that Theodor began to have doubts about his teaching manual, and felt inclined to let his pupil's errors stand uncorrected. Things had always been like that. Theodor had always believed in external power, in any external power which faced him. Only in the army was he happy. There he had to believe what was told him, and others had to believe what he himself told them. Theodor would gladly have spent his whole life in the army.

Civilian life was different. It was harsh, and full of hidden traps in unknown corners. One made an effort but found no target for it, one wasted energy on uncertainties, it was like ceaselessly building houses of cards only for unforeseeable gusts of wind to blow them down. No effort was of any use, no amount of hard work was rewarded. There was no superior whose mood one could divine or whose wishes one could foresee. Everybody was a superior, all the people in the street, all the classmates in the lecture room, mothers and sisters too.

Everyone had an easy life; the Glasers and the Efrussis the easiest of all. Glaser was top of the heap, along with the rich jeweller and the jeweller's son. In the army they had amounted to nothing, had rarely even made sergeant. There, justice defeated sharp practice. And everything was sharp practice. Glaser's learning was as dishonestly come by as the jeweller's fortune. There was something wrong with things when Private Grunbaum was granted leave or when Efrussi made a deal. The revolution was a swindle, the Kaiser had been betrayed, the Republic was a Jewish conspiracy. Theodor could see all this for himself, and other people's opinions confirmed his impressions. Clever men like Wilhelm Tieckmann, Professor Koethe, Bastelmann the lecturer, the physicist Lorranz and the ethnologist Mannheim all made a point of exposing the harmful nature of the Jewish race during lecture evenings at the Union of German Law Students, as well as in their own books, which were on display in the reading room of the 'Germania'.

Father Lohse had often enough warned his daughters against any contact with young Jews during their dancing classes. He could give examples, yes, examples! At least twice a month, Jews from Posen, the worst of the lot, would try to cheat him. During the war they had been classified as unfit for active service, and were to be found as writers in field hospitals and area headquarters.

In the seminars on jurisprudence they would always push themselves forward and think up new conundrums, in which Theodor would find himself all at sea and which would drive him to new, disagreeable and difficult labours.

They had destroyed the army now, they had taken over the State, discovered socialism and that one should love one's enemy. It was written in *The Elders of Zion* – a book which was issued to the officer reservists on Fridays, along with the vegetables – that they aimed at world dominion. They had the police in their pockets and were persecuting the nationalist organisations. And one was reduced to educating their sons, to living off them, badly. And how did they themselves live?

Oh! They lived in style. The Efrussi mansion was separated from the common street by a shining, silvery railing, and surrounded by a broad, green lawn. The gravel gleamed white and the steps up to the door were even whiter. Pictures in gold frames hung in the hall and a footman in green and gold livery bowed as he escorted you in. The jeweller was lank and tall, and always wore black, with a high-collared coat which just revealed a black silk stock pinned by a pearl the size of a hazelnut.

Theodor's family lived in three rooms in Moabit, the handsomest of which contained two rickety cupboards, with a sideboard as showpiece and, as solitary decoration, the silver dish which Theodor had salvaged from the château at Amiens, and which he had hidden in the bottom of his trunk in the nick of time, just before the arrival of the stern Major Krause, who did not allow that kind of thing.

No! Theodor did not live in a villa behind silver-gleaming wrought-iron railings, and no high rank consoled him for the poverty of his life. He was a tutor whose hopes had miscarried, whose courage had been buried, but whose ambition was eternally present to torment him. Women, with the sweet rhythm of their swaying hips, passed by him, unattainable, but he was still on fire to possess them. He would have had them all, as a lieutenant, even young Frau Efrussi, the jeweller's second wife.

How remote she was, coming from that great world to which Theodor might have belonged. She was a lady: Jewish, but a lady. He should have met her in the uniform of a lieutenant, not in the civilian clothes of a tutor. During his days as a lieutenant, on leave in Berlin, he did once have an adventure with a lady. One could call her a lady; she was the wife of a cigar merchant who was away in Flanders. His photograph was hanging in the dining room, and she wore

7

violet knickers. These were the first violet knickers of Theodor's masculine existence.

What inkling had he now of women? His were the cheap little girls, the hurried minutes of cold love in the darkness of a vestibule, or in some alcove, haunted by the fear that the neighbours might come home unexpectedly, the pleasure which died away at the sound of an unexpected footstep and the glow of warmth which cooled off, raw and wet. His was the barefoot simpleton from the north, the woman with the angular rough hands and the crude caresses, chill to the touch, with sweaty stockings and dirty underclothes.

Frau Efrussi was not of his world. As he listened to her, it occurred to him that she must be a good person. No one had ever said such beautiful things to him with such simplicity and sincerity. You understand perfectly, Herr Lohse! Do you like this place? Are you comfortable with us? Oh, she was such a good person, so beautiful and so young. Theodor could have wished for a sister like her.

He was startled once, when he suddenly saw her coming out of a shop; it was as if he had had a revelation. He realised that all during his walk he had been thinking of her. It frightened him so much to discover that she lived within him that he stopped unconsciously in his tracks, accepted her invitation to ride in her car without being aware of it, and almost got in before her. He bumped against her several times, touched her arm and hastily apologised. He hardly heard her questions. He had to concentrate hard on not touching her again. But it happened again, nonetheless. He prepared anxiously for the moment when he would leave the car, but it stopped sooner than he had expected and there was no chance to get out and hand her down. He remained seated and by the time he had got out and down the chauffeur already held the parcel he was proposing to carry for her.

From a great distance he heard her say goodbye, but her smile was inescapably close before his eyes, like the reflected smile of a woman far away.

He would never reach her. Did he indeed wish to? He did, ardently. But now that he was no longer a lieutenant, his belief in his own power to make the first move had gone. He would have had to have his rank back. He longed to be a lieutenant again. A lieutenant, or at least something, not to be anonymous, a nobody, a modest brick in a wall, the least of a group of comrades, the one who listened and laughed when anecdotes were told and dirty stories bandied about. He longed not to be alone any more in the midst of so many, alone with his vain longing to make himself heard and to be done with the eternal disappointment of not being listened to and being tolerated and even popular because of his grateful attentiveness. Ah, they thought he was harmless. They would see! Everyone would see! Soon he would come out of his corner, a conqueror, no longer trapped in time, no longer crushed to the ground by the weight of his days. Somewhere on the horizon, bright fanfares sounded.

2

At times his pride overcame him, like some alien power, and he was afraid of his own wishes, which held him in thrall. But as soon as he walked through the streets he heard a million unknown voices, and a million motley colours dazzled him, the treasures of the world ringing and shining. Music drifted from open windows, sweet scent from women passing by, pride and power from confident men. Every time he passed through the Brandenburg Gate he dreamed the old lost dream of his triumphal entry on a snow white horse, a captain at the head of his company, under the eyes of thousands of women, perhaps kissed by some, flags fluttering, deafened by cheers. He had carried this dream in his heart and had fed it lovingly ever since he had first reported to barracks as a volunteer, through all the deprivations and mortal dangers of war. The painful dressings-down by the sergeant-major on the parade ground had been made less harsh by this dream, as had the daylong hunger of the endless march, the burning pain in his knees, confinement in a dark cell, the blinding, painful whiteness of the outpost in the snow, the biting frost in his toes.

His dream cried out for release, like some sickness living invisibly in his joints, nerves and muscles, filling every blood vessel, which he could no more escape than he could escape himself. And, in accordance with that unknown power which had often before helped Theodor, and which had taught him that, at the last moment, some helpful external circumstance would come halfway towards fulfilling any painful dream, so it happened that in the Efrussis' house he made the acquaintance of Dr Trebitsch.

For the first quarter of an hour of their acquaintance, Dr Trebitsch never stopped talking, and his beard, which was fair and long and fell in soft locks, edged with highlights, moved up and down before Theodor's eyes so regularly as to destroy his concentration. The words of the fair-bearded doctor pattered softly down, here and there a word or two would catch Theodor's attention for an instant and then float away again. He had never been at such close quarters with a spade beard. Suddenly, the sound of a name shook him out of his stupefied abstraction. It was the name of Prince Heinrich. With the instinct of a man who comes by chance across a prize piece from his shattered past and clutches it hastily to his bosom, Theodor cried: 'I was a lieutenant in the regiment of His Highness, Prince Heinrich!'

'The Prince will be very pleased,' said Dr Trebitsch, and his voice was no longer distant, but very, very close.

Pride, like something physical, filled Theodor's chest and puffed out his stiff shirt. They drove by car to the mess and, unlike the previous week when he had driven with Frau Efrussi, he did not feel cowed and scrawny, hunched in the corner between the side of the car and the upholstered seat. He expanded. Through his overcoat, his tailcoat and his white waistcoat his body was aware of the cool, yielding softness of the leather. He propped his feet against the seat in front. His cigar filled the coupé with the satisfying aroma of an overflowing sense of comfort. He opened the window and felt the swift, penetratingly cold March air with the delight of someone who was warm to the depths of his being. They were drinking schnaps and beer, and the evening in the mess reminded him of the Kaiser's birthday. Count Straubwitz of the Cuirassiers made a speech and they gave him three cheers. Someone told anecdotes from the war. Theodor was seated as a guest next to the Prince. He didn't take his eyes off His Highness for a moment. He ignored the guest on his other side. It was imperative that he be ready at any moment to answer the Prince's questions. Not for one moment did Theodor forget that now he had the chance to realise at least part of his dream. Was he now the unknown little tutor of a Jewish boy? Did not the Prince know him? Was he not known to all the gentlemen seated round this table? And, although the unaccustomed alcohol gradually dulled Theodor's awareness of the evening's minor realities, yet a great happiness lingered in him and a sense of self-assurance came back to him each time he handed the Prince a table napkin, a glass, or a light for his cigarette.

At the Prince's request he described the battle near Stojanowics at which the regiment had so distinguished itself. He began somewhat at random, and in a rather louder tone of voice than usual. At first things went along all right, until he noticed that he had begun his tale before deciding how he was going to end it. He paused, and the deep, attentive silence shattered him. He only knew that his previous phrase had been: 'Captain von der Heidt!' 'So this captain,' he began again, but he never finished the sentence. 'Long live von der Heidt! Cheers!' broke in Dr Trebitsch, and they all drank to the gallant captain.

It then turned out that Theodor and the Prince went the same way home, so they sat together in the car. Theodor talked as they drove. Frau Efrussi came into his head and he told the Prince about her. He could see her green eyes, and her shoulders. He peeled off her clothes and she was standing before him in her underclothes. She was wearing violet knickers. He told the Prince about everything he saw, did, and felt. 'I slipped her blouse off,' said Theodor. 'Your Highness should know that she has brown nipples, and that I bit her firm breasts.'

'You're a great lad,' said the Prince.

He used this expression again later as they sat in his room drinking yet another black coffee, yet another liqueur. They sat side by side, so close to each other that their calves touched and the Prince was holding Theodor's hand and squeezing it. And all at once Theodor was naked and so was Prince Heinrich. The Prince had a richly matted chest and skinny legs. He was slightly pigeon-toed. Theodor's head was bowed, and although it was distressing to him, he was obliged to look at these toes. It occurred to him that it would be better by far to look the Prince in the eye. The Prince was squeezing a cool, fine-scented spray from a little rubber ball.

For the first time Theodor saw himself stark naked in a tall pier mirror. He could observe that his skin was white and rose-tinted, that his legs were roundly fashioned, his chest a little arched, his nipples like two bright little dark red cupolas.

Theodor was lying on the warm, soft polar-bear skin and beside him lay Prince Heinrich, breathing heavily and audibly. The Prince bit into Theodor's flesh. The stubble of the Prince's beard was scratchy, and the tangled hair of his chest and legs tickled Theodor.

He awoke to a half-dark room, and the first thing to meet his gaze was a portrait in oils of the Prince hanging on the wall. Horribly awake, he saw all the events of the night before. He fought against them in vain. He tried to erase them. They had simply not taken place. He began to think of all sorts of unrelated matters. He conjugated a Greek verb. But his most recent experiences set about him like a persistent swarm of flies. He walked slowly down the stairs, to be greeted by an ancient and respectful servant. The world's proximity was audible already in the merry ringing of a tram bell.

Oh, how near he was to this rich world, with its million treasures ringing and shining. He was experiencing the streets, the way the women walked with swaying hips, the men striding with assurance, and he himself, so small and so inadequate in their midst.

He would be leaving the house, a man smaller than ever before. It had always been like this, that he had to retrace his steps, mortified, just as he had felt himself exalted, that he must in his loneliness take paths which led downwards just as he was about to storm the heights. He did not want to turn back, he wanted to stay here. And so he stood before the old servant and asked after the Prince.

Prince Heinrich was eating breakfast, his feet in a footwarmer placed beneath the table. 'Morning, Theo!' he said, and left Theodor standing.

Theodor came quite close to the table and studied the Prince.

The Prince broke egg after egg and threw the yolks into a glass.

'Sit down,' he said at last. And, as if it had just occurred to him: 'Have you eaten yet?' and pushed eggs, bread and butter over to Theodor.

The food strengthened Theodor. He ate in silence and a good, restorative, innocent peace enfolded him.

Suddenly, as if his tongue had declared its entire independence of him, his question flew across the table: would the Prince have any use for a secretary?

Prince Heinrich nodded. He had long been expecting the question. He wrote something on a visiting card: 'Trebitsch,' said the Prince; nothing more. And as Theodor rose to his feet: 'Morning!'

And Theodor rose to his feet and walked out into the fresh, March morning, through the Tiergarten, breathing in the blue of the sky and the first bird calls, in the knowledge that he was climbing upwards although the street was level. And he knew that one has to pass through the depths and that one should forget them. He would put aside the distracting recollections of the previous night, now swallowed up by the brilliant blue of morning.

3

Trebitsch received him and, by ceremonial candlelight, Theodor swore a long oath and set his name to a sheet of paper whose contents he had scarcely looked at. For two minutes his hand lay in the hairy paw of a man who was referred to as Detective Klitsche, and who was to be his instructor. A long and inadequate lock of this man's hair fell across an earlobe which had been shot off or otherwise tampered with. Theodor was now a member of an organisation, a society, the name of which he did not know. All he knew was a letter and a Roman numeral – the letter S and the numeral II – and that the centre of this unknown group was situated in Munich. He was to await verbal or written instructions from Klitsche. To obey orders under all circumstances was a condition, as was silence. Betrayal meant death and an ill-considered statement meant certain destruction.

In spite of his own wishes, and in defiance of his reflective temperament, things were moving too fast for Theodor. He was repeatedly stopped short by all these new experiences, and felt that he had been overtaken by events. He was frightened by the lighted candles and the resounding phrases of the oath, and by the hairy paw of his superior. He was as conscious of the nearness of death as was any traitor newly condemned. He had never been a bad sleeper; his dreams were few, but comforting. Before going to sleep, he used to paint himself beautiful pictures of the future, even if the day which was ending had given him no cause for encouragement. After that morning in Dr Trebitsch's office, he began dreaming of candles burning yellow in the full light of day. Worst of all was the thought that there was no escape, and that he could no longer return to the sheltered quiet of a tutor's life, a life of freedom. What orders were awaiting him? Murder, robbery and perilous espionage? How many enemies lurked in the darkness of the evening streets? He was no longer assured even of his life.

But what rewards could be his! Skipping the time during which I am imprisoned in the dark gaol of this existence, I throw off the heavy yoke of these days, I rise up and shatter closed doors, I, Theodor Lohse, a man in danger but a dangerous man, more than a lieutenant, more than a victor on horseback, riding through cheering crowds; the saviour of my country, perhaps. In these times victory is for the daring.

A day or two later he received his first orders: to give notice at the Efrussis and to cash a cheque, for a fantastic sum, signed by Heinrich Meyer, at the Dresdner Bank. Theodor had never had so much money about him, and the awareness of it altered his expression, his walk, the way he held himself and the whole world around him. It was a clear April evening, the girls had light dresses and lively breasts. Every window at the front of every house stood open. Twittering sparrows hopped between piles of yellow horse-dung. The streets were smiling. The lamplighter was already wearing his white summer overall. The world was unquestionably growing younger. The last rays of the sun quivered in little puddles of mire. The girls smiled and seemed approachable. There were blonde ones and brunettes and black-haired ones. But that was a superficial division. Girls with wide hips were Theodor's special delight. He loved to find a refuge and a home in women. After the consummation he liked to be mothered by the all-embracing, to lay his head between big, kindly breasts.

It was the sort of day on which it would be easy to give notice to the Efrussis. He had first come to their house two years before, to the day, and now he would never see young Frau Efrussi again. He thought of her as of a landscape once glimpsed afar off, in which one could never linger.

He could perhaps give his notice in writing – on some pretext or other. Exams were now taking up so much of his time. But that would not only be a lie, but a cowardly one, and the chance would be missed to tell the detested Efrussi the truth which he had painfully bitten back for so long.

'Herr Efrussi, I am a poor German and you are a rich Jew. It is treachery to eat the bread of a Jew.'

But Theodor did not speak like that to the dark, haggard Efrussi, whose face recalled the portrait of a stern old lady. He simply said: 'I would like to inform you of something, Herr Efrussi.'

'Please do,' said Efrussi.

'I have been teaching in your house for two years now . . .'

'I will raise your salary,' interrupted Efrussi.

'No, on the contrary. I am giving notice,' said Theodor.

'What for?'

'Because in fact Herr Trebitsch . . .'

Efrussi smiled: 'Look here, Herr Lohse, I have known Trebitsch for a very long time. His father was a business friend of my father's. He was a big man in manufacturing, and an important one. His son would have done better to stay with the business. I know Dr Trebitsch's little games. You are the third tutor he has taken from me. He is a devious fool.'

'He is a friend of His Highness, Prince Heinrich.'

'Yes,' said Efrussi, 'the Prince is known to have many friends.'

17

'What do you mean by that? I was a lieutenant in the Prince's regiment.'

'The Prince's regiment was certainly a gallant one. Generally speaking, I am strongly in favour of principalities, but very little in favour of princes. But that is neither here nor there.'

'But then,' said Theodor, without having grasped the implications of Efrussi's last phrase, 'but then, you are a Jew!'

'Nothing new in that for me.' Efrussi smiled. 'Trebitsch is a Jew, too; not that I have any wish to make comparisons. But I do understand you. I read the national press. I even advertise in the *Deutsche Zeitung*. So you don't want to go on teaching my son. Here is your pay for last month. Let nothing deter you from accepting it. It is yours by right!'

Theodor took it. Any hesitation on his part would have prolonged the discussion. And was it not, indeed, his by right? Had he not the better part of three weeks in the current month behind him? He took the money, bowed and went.

He didn't know that Efrussi immediately rang up Major Pauli at garrison headquarters to complain of the loss of his tutor. 'You're carrying this *agent provocateur* business too far!' said Efrussi; and the major apologised.

But Theodor has carried out his first instructions. He has taken away with him a bleeding heart. He will never see Frau Efrussi again.

And it seems to him that now, for the first time, he has honoured his long, resounding oath. This giving of his notice was a door slammed, the end of a journey, the end of a life.

4

For three days and nights Theodor enjoyed his money without a thought. He slept with girls off the streets and with more expensive ones who were lurking in the clubs. He drank wine which he did not enjoy, and sweet liqueurs which upset his stomach and the horrible taste of which he tried to dispel with cognac. He slept in grubby rooming houses only to discover later that for the same price he could have had all the paradisal pleasures of a big hotel. He joined, once, his former comrades in arms, bought them a couple of rounds and was then mocked by them. Each setback to his pursuit of pleasure stung his pride, and only fear of his fatal oath restrained him from divulging his secret and stifled the words on his rebellious lips: I, Theodor Lohse, am a member of a secret organisation.

How they would admire him, if they but knew! But almost as precious as admiration was the secret with which he lived, and his disguise. He was about to manipulate the invisible threads from which, as he knew from the newspapers, ministers, civil servants, statesmen and officials depended. And all the time he was assuming the unlikely cloak of a law student and a private tutor. He could pass a policeman and remain unrecognised. No one could see how dangerous he was. It sometimes occurred to him to reinforce his own invisibility, and he would step for a few minutes into some dark hallway and make believe that he was watching someone without being seen. He prepared himself for his new profession by carrying out missions he devised himself. He would go into one ministry or another and ask for an imaginary person. He would read the names of the officials over the porter's shoulder as he searched, and then walk contentedly away. He began to take note of things which had never interested him. He bought revolutionary broadsheets, he went into the offices of the *Red Flag* to place some insignificant small advertisement and noted how easily penetrated the place was. They should be pleased with him. Should someone give him an assignment, he would already know how to go about a number of important procedures.

He devoted the strenuous energy which he had once given to his entry into barracks life to accomplish imaginary assignments and unrequired tasks. Certainly, it was easier in the army, because one was more closely supervised. One knew the NCO in charge of the dormitory, and the lecturers, the sergeants and the sergeant-major. But here one was working in the dark. Should one carry out one's duties on behalf of Trebitsch or Detective Klitsche? It was hard to tell.

Theodor went aimlessly about the streets, filled with a restless, unharnessed zeal. He felt the need to define a visible territory for his activities, and to achieve undeniable successes. He stopped in front of a photographer's display window on Unter den Linden. Here hung a coloured photograph of General Ludendorff, a showpiece of the photographer's skill. Theodor had always made every effort to come into contact with the high and the mighty. Even in school, by means of all sorts of little services and demonstrations of respect, he had seen to it that the teacher would favour him with some personal task during break. During the war he had become, after a few short months, adjutant to the colonel. Looking at Ludendorff's portrait, Theodor stumbled on the idea of using his old methods again and establishing contact with the general. His heart thumped, his blood beat in his temples, just as if he were standing before the general in person, not merely before his photograph. He went into a café and wrote a respectful letter to 'Ludendorff, Munich,' without any more detailed address, trusting to the general's fame and the reliability of the post.

And he received an answer. He read it and grew, word by short metallic word. 'Dear friend,' wrote the general, 'I like you. Be zealous for God, Freedom and Fatherland. Yours, Ludendorff.'

Theodor read the letter over and over: in the tram, at the tram stop, in college and while he ate. Even on the street and in the traffic's whirlpool the desire to read the letter overcame him. It drew him to one of those little benches perched at the edge of a piece of lawn. He had never sat on one before, because of his revulsion for this plebeian form of seating and the members of the lower orders who used it. On this occasion he was miles away from the people with whom he was sharing the bench. He read the letter, wandered away and, ten minutes later, came back and sat down again.

Like a pious commentator on Holy Writ, Theodor was constantly finding new interpretations for the general's letter. He soon persuaded himself that the general was aware of Theodor Lohse's entry into the secret organisation. Trebitsch must have informed him. Was Theodor not a personal friend of the Prince? Between the despatch of the letter and the arrival of the answer eight days had passed. Ludendorff had therefore sent to Berlin for the information. 'My dear friend,' the general had written. This is the manner in which one writes to someone who promises more for the future than he has accomplished so far.

Theodor went to the 'Germania'. In the reading room, Spitz, the expert on German affairs, was giving a lecture on racial problems. Wilhelm Tiedemann and others from the Association of German Law Students were present. Tiedemann read the letter. In his view, Theodor could rely on it. And Tiedemann was as much convinced as Theodor was that Ludendorff must have been aware of his new friend's personality.

Everyone told Theodor so. They were all his friends. Every eye was a loving eye. He could hear the beat of every heart, and the beat of their hearts was the language of friendship. He stood them drinks. He put his arm round Tiedemann's shoulder. Everyone drank at Theodor's expense. They toasted him. He talked a lot, and a lot more occurred to him. When he left he carried with him the mighty sound of his own words.

The following morning brought him an invitation to call on Detective Klitsche. He was not to write a letter of any sort, and least of all to Ludendorff. He should never have talked about it. He was not the only person in the Association of German Law Students to belong to the organisation, and every word he had uttered yesterday had been reported to Klitsche.

'Hand over the letter!' said Klitsche.

Theodor went red. Fiery wheels spun before his eyes. He was suddenly the little first-year recruit standing on the barracks square. He stood stiffly to attention in the approved manner. He was a little first-year man with his eye on his first stripe.

He handed over the letter. Klitsche pocketed it. He ordered: 'Take your clothes off!'

And Theodor took his clothes off. He took his clothes off as if it were quite a matter of routine. He thought to himself that he had to obey Klitsche.

Slowly and indifferently he put his clothes back on again, as slowly and as indifferently as he had put them on in his room every morning.

In the streets it was spring, birds twittered, the trams rang their bells, the sky was blue, the women were wearing light dresses.

Theodor would have liked to be ill, and a little boy, in his bed. He drank in second-class drinking shops and slept with girls from the Potsdamer Platz because his money was beginning to run out, and when he had none left he found the noisy gaiety of the streets a thousand times stronger in comparison to his own insignificance. And he forgot his visit to Klitsche, just as he had buried his visit to Prince Heinrich. His way led over precipices and into chasms.

5

For the time being, his way led to the residence of the painter, Klaften.

Theodor called himself Friedrich Trattner, a comrade from Hamburg. At Klaften's he saw modern pictures, fanfaronades of tearing colours, yellow, violet, red. Looking away from the pictures, his eyes smarted as if one had been looking into the sun. Theodor said: 'Really beautiful!'

His admiration took care of everything and made people accept his identity. They addressed him as Comrade Trattner. He carried his new name with a flourish. He, who was surprised, and could be shaken, by any new situation, now invented his own: adventurous escapes from prison, sudden flight on the appearance of spies, set-tos with the police and students.

Theodor grew into the part of Friedrich Trattner. Through the person of this figure he acquired respect and stature. It was like being a temporary NCO in the army who had to be thoroughly tested out before he could go any further. This was soon got over. One was at pains to be worthy of one's new rank, but only so as to be able to be free of it.

Theodor made the acquaintance of new people: the Jew Goldscheider, who preached goodness and quoted the New Testament at every opportunity. Was he a Bolshevik or just a Jew? Goldscheider himself described his stay in a lunatic asylum. He was certainly foolish, at times incomprehensible. The others pretended to understand. This was a harmless company of poor young men without a roof over their heads. They found lodgings and a coffee at Klaften's place. The painter made his living from conventional paintings, which were generally regarded in that company as *kitsch*. Theodor reckoned they were Klaften's best work.

Theodor heard these young people cursing. They saw the great revolution almost within their grasp. They cursed socialist ministers and officials whom Theodor had always held to be communists. The fine distinctions escaped him.

Klaften made a portrait of him. Theodor was afraid of his own picture. It was as if he looked into a terrifying mirror. His face was round and reddish, his nose flattened, with faintly indicated cracks on the flat bridge. The mouth was wide, with broad, open, shovel-like lips. In reality his small moustache hid his lips, but not in the painting. It was as though the painter had shaved off his beard – and yet he had painted it in.

It hasn't worked, thought Theodor. The picture hung in the room and betrayed him. Everyone seeing the picture fell silent and looked stealthily at Theodor, who felt himself stripped of his mask, and would have run from the picture had it not been for the arrival of Thimme, a young communist.

Thimme had stored explosives in a safe rooming house, in the cellar. He wanted to set it off in the service of the revolution. He spoke of the need for a new revolutionary act and found everyone in agreement and Theodor especially enthusiastic.

Theodor was all ears and wished he were all arms. He thought of that spider from his boyhood days, which he used to feed each day with captured flies. He remembered waiting breathlessly as the creature climbed its web, how it watched for a second before making its final deadly rush, which was assault, leap and drop all in one movement.

He himself now sat like that, ready for the attack, determined to spring. He hated these people without knowing why, but fabricated his own reasons for hating them. They were socialists, without belief in a Fatherland, traitors. They were in his power. Yes, he held in his power five, six, or ten men. He held power over men again, he, Theodor Lohse, the private tutor, the law student, who had been made to look small by Detective Klitsche, who had been misused by the Prince and betrayed by his comrades. Everyone could see the fire in his eyes and the colour in his cheeks. He looked at Thimme, the young and hungry Thimme. He was a glass-blower, patently tubercular, who bore the darkness of death in his deeply shadowed eyes. He looked on Thimme as his prey, his man, his own.

He relished his concealment as if it were some nourishing food. He edged back into the darkness. He flexed his fingers in his trouser pockets and stooped forward from the waist. He assumed, unconsciously, the threatening posture of the spider.

They argued about the objective to be attacked. Some favoured the Reichstag, others the police, and others the Kaiser-Wilhelm-Gedächtnis church. Goldscheider stood with outstretched arms and begged and besought them not to touch the explosives. He had taken off his spectacles and his bearded face looked lost, helpless and in need of rescue.

Who was to make the attempt? They decided to draw lots. It fell to Goldscheider.

Theodor left. Late in the night he left the house, and strode through the dark and rustling Tiergarten to Trebitsch. He slipped through the last avenue as if he were being pursued, hugging the dark shadows of the trees. He didn't want to wake anyone. He threw a pebble at Trebitsch's lighted window. He went in, looking over his shoulder at the door. He described the immense danger he was in. Spies had followed him here, communist spies, and on the way he had leapt onto a bus. They were beginning to suspect him. They doubted that his name was really Trattner. And, as he told his tale, his fear increased. He was no longer the cunning infiltrator as he described his anxious imaginings. 'Explosives,' he said softly, and looked towards the door.

'They should not be disturbed,' said Trebitsch softly, smiling as always, and running his fingers through his beard as if they were a comb. After the attack — and it was to be hoped that it would succeed — the police would have to be briefed.

At about four in the morning Theodor went back to the painter Klaften's place. They had decided on the Victory Column. Two of them had brought the explosives in a taxi. Thimme bored a hole in the box. Thimme, Theodor and Goldscheider drove to the Column. Thimme and Theodor waited at a convenient distance. All three of them walked away, silent and grim.

Fifteen minutes after Goldscheider had lit the fuse, Theodor called the police: in a few minutes there would be a disaster. Behind the railings surrounding the Victory Column, and to the right of it, there were explosives.

Goldscheider went back to Klaften's place — the police seized him and bound him, swiftly and silently. Out of the room, handcuffed two by two, came the comrades. Beside the police inspector stood Trattner, Comrade Trattner.

They all spat at once, as if at a command, and before they could be prevented, right in his face.

Theodor wiped the spittle off it with his handkerchief. He laughed, shortly, but loud and deep. It sounded almost like a cry.

In the hallway, the dazzling torches of the police went out. From the street one could hear the ten prisoners marching in step, and the light, metallic sound of handcuffs rubbing together.

6

Sensational headlines in the newspapers: 'Communist Attack Thwarted by Member of the Technical Emergency Service!' Theodor Lohse was mentioned by name a few times. People congratulated him. He became a rare visitor to the Association of German Law Students. He no longer went to his lectures. There would be time for all that later on.

He hadn't seen his name in print since he had been mentioned in despatches. Now he came across his name in all the papers. A man came from the *Nationale Beobachter*, a thin little man who fiddled all the time with odds and ends on the writing table while he spoke. He invited Theodor to co-operate exclusively with the paper, at the same time making it clear that its budget did not, unfortunately, extend to paying a fee.

What did that matter? Theodor had received a fee from Trebitsch, rather higher than his original one. And that had been split in half because Klitsche demanded his cut. It was he who had put Theodor on to the painter Klaften! He, Klitsche, had taken himself off the case out of unselfish friendship for Theodor. Klitsche sat in his office with his coat and waistcoat off and his collar open, looking more powerful than ever. One could see his bull neck with its prominent muscles, and his clenched and heavy fists as they rested on the desk. His lank strands of hair had been pushed back and revealed the flawed remains of his ear muscles, all reddish gristle and atrophied whorls. Theodor haggled bitterly, only wanting to give him a third, but Klitsche had pushed back his chair with sudden determination, as if about to get to his feet. He did not do so, but stayed in the chair which he had pushed back, his torso leaning forward, a crouching beast; and Theodor gave him half. He then walked through the streets, stopped in front of a shop window and bought a pair of boots. He had the impression of having grown taller, of treading fresh ground underfoot.

Late in the afternoon, as the birds were singing their sweet evening songs, he spoke to a girl in a white dress. In the course of the evening they visited a *palais de danse*, and he was jealous because the girl danced three times in a row with a man from a neighbouring table. He was drinking sour *sekt*. The girl – one could hardly call her that – demanded a better hotel, and forced Theodor to book two rooms. Then he was not to come to her for fifteen minutes, after which he knocked on the door, listened, knocked again and went in. The girl had disappeared.

He had more luck with young women who went hatless, in simple blouses and threadbare coats. These were satisfied with a visit to the cinema. He was careful not to let these little distractions develop into lasting friendships, and he made a point of never making definite dates.

He was pleased with himself and convinced that willpower and talent had made possible his modest progress in so short a time.

He felt that he had happened upon the one occupation to which he was really suited. He was proud of his ability as a spy and thought of himself as a diplomat. His interest in all things criminal increased. He would sit in the cinema by the hour. He took to reading detective stories.

There still lived within him the portrait which Klaften had made of him. He tried to make a lie of it. He grew his moustache bushier. He changed his style of dress. Nowadays he wore a light brown suit, or a pale green check, with a small gold swastika pin in a silk tie with diagonal stripes.

He bought all sorts of weapons, a leather cosh, a pistol, a rubber truncheon. Like Detective Klitsche, he never went anywhere without a revolver, and in every passer-by he saw a communist spy. He knew he was not really being followed, but he would forget, especially after seeing a spy thriller. It flattered him to think of being followed, so he would believe it.

He, for whom every new hour had seemed frightening simply because it was new, who had feared the future and loved the familiar, now toyed with bold improbabilities and anticipated adventure at every step. He was armoured.

He began to be sceptical. Behind each plain fact he saw

29

veils which concealed secrets and the true state of things. He read politico-philosophical tracts which Trebitsch had published: broadsheets in which links between socialism, Jewry, France and Russia were disclosed. This reading fed Theodor's fantasies. Not only did he believe what he read, but from this material he construed new facts and expounded them in the *Nationale Beobachter*. Being in print made his self-confidence grow, and when his pen was in his hand he no longer doubted the truth of what he had carefully prepared himself to set down. Once he had read his manuscript over, he became certain, and struck out all the qualifying phrases, every 'perhaps', every 'probably'. He wrote essays like one who has glimpsed the corridors of power.

He knew that the *Nationale Beobachter* lay about in the reading rooms of the 'Germania', and that Tiedemann and the others read it. The *Nationale Beobachter* hung in the kiosks of the Underground, at every street corner, and from every kiosk and every street corner the red and white front page shouted the name of Theodor Lohse to the world.

He no longer envied the Efrussis their gleaming white house beyond green lawn, the silver railings and the marble steps. He thought of the lost Frau Efrussi in the way that a great man thinks of an ordinary woman who has provided him with a little adventure. He did not envy Efrussi, but he hated him, his tribe, his pride and the way in which he had, at the finish, treated him, the tutor. Theodor now recalled that in the house of the Efrussis he had adopted a modest mien, that he had in those days been governed by stupid anxiety; and he blamed the Jew for it. It was the Jews who were responsible for his long years without success; it was they who had prevented him from discovering the world earlier! At school it had been Glaser, the exceptional student, and other Jews – whose names he could not recall – had come later. They were, as the whole world knew, formidable, because they held power. But they were also hateful and repulsive, wherever they turned up – in the tram, on the street, at the theatre. And Theodor, when he saw a Jew, would pointedly finger his tie, so as to draw the other's attention to the threatening *swastika* pin. The Jews did not bat an eyelid, thereby proving their impertinence. They looked indifferently at Theodor, sometimes even sneered at him, and then swore at him when he demanded satisfaction.

He was infuriated, and sometimes, at night, he would abuse passers-by in quiet streets and, when danger threatened, disappear down side turnings. It so happened that he told Detective Klitsche and Dr Trebitsch about these adventures. Instead of praising him, as he had expected, they told him to discipline himself, because people who belonged to an organisation must not draw attention to themselves. From then on he kept silence, but hatred gnawed at him, and found its outlet through articles in the *Nationale Beobachter*. These articles became ever more virulent, until the paper was banned for a month, specifically because of an article by Theodor Lohse. Several younger readers wrote to congratulate him on his success. Women, too, wrote to him. Theodor answered them. People called on him. Boys just out of high school, members of the *Bismarck-Bund*, sent him invitations, looked up to him, watched him attentively, a silent, chosen Master. He gave lectures and stood on the podium amid the surging applause of his followers. He founded a National Youth League, and went into the woods on Sundays with his youngsters and taught them drill.

But he was short of cash, and there was no prospect of earning more: these were quiet times. No more plain-clothes men were to be seen in Detective Klitsche's office. Klitsche was not in any case assigned any. He was on the payroll and

31

in constant touch with Munich. Theodor would have been glad of a similar posting. He did not care for Klitsche. Klitsche was an obstacle. This Klitsche had been a sergeant-major, while Theodor, after all, had been a lieutenant, and was an educated man. Sometimes he hinted as much to Trebitsch. 'Perhaps Klitsche will drop dead!' Trebitsch once said in jest. Since that day Theodor had thought about Klitsche's death. But Klitsche was fit. He proved it at every meeting, with every handshake, with his Homeric laughter. There was no hope of Klitsche being summoned to Munich, or giving any grounds for reproach.

Now and again, Theodor thought of somehow betraying Klitsche. How? Was it impossible? Didn't Klitsche associate with communist agents? Who kept an eye on him? Who knew him really well? Surely an observant watcher could catch him out?

For the time being, it was impossible, and Theodor needed money. An attempt to prise a loan out of Trebitsch misfired. He not only explained that he himself was in debt, but also suggested other, richer men of Theodor's acquaintance: for example the Prince.

'You're a friend of the Prince's!' said Trebitsch.

Yes, he was a friend of the Prince's, and wasn't the Prince still under an obligation to him?

He went to Prince Heinrich. He had to wait a long time, because it was afternoon and the Prince was sleeping. Finally he appeared, in flowered silk pyjamas, his cheeks and dimples rosy from sleep, like a child on waking.

'Ah! Theo!' said the Prince.

He sat down, put one foot on the table, let his slippers drop off and watched his toes as he wriggled them. He hummed a little tune, and yawned from time to time. He did not listen to everything Theodor said. Finally, he interrupted him. 'You can come with me to Königsberg, to the launching,' he said.

So Theodor, wearing a dazzling white sailor's cap, travelled in a first-class compartment to Königsberg. His Highness, the Prince, slept on the way, a book by Heinz Torote dangling from his right hand. The *Deutsche Treue* rowing club came to meet them, fed them and put them up. Next day they stood by the water. It was a Sunday, and it was raining, as is customary at launchings. A girl dressed in white was holding a glass of wine in her right hand and an umbrella in her left. The prince stepped up to the boat, bestowed his name and smashed the glass against its side. Everybody cried hip, hip, hooray! and the rain poured down.

In the afternoon they inspected a guard of honour from the *Reichswehr*, and made the acquaintance of the *Rhenania* students' association. Theodor recognised the student Günther as a comrade from the war. They drank together, wandered round the town, related their experiences, thought themselves fine fellows and put their arms around each other. Now there were no secrets between them, and Theodor withheld only the nature of his relationship with the Prince and Klitsche. Even so, just once, he did mention their names, and Günther admitted that he, too, belonged to Branch S II in Munich, and received missions from Klitsche. But he was sick of politics now and wanted to marry. And yes, he would go to Berlin with Theodor. He longed for it.

His fiancée was a workman's daughter, her father a shop steward at the Schuckert works. Just a plain workman, and a red.

Theodor asked if Günther were half red. He kept his hands in his pockets, stretched his fingers and listened, all ears.

'No!' But he did talk with his future father-in-law in a non-committal sort of way.

They travelled together; the Prince slept in a nearby compartment and Theodor kept silence. He watched the

33

landscape. He looked at Günther, a straw-haired, blue-eyed youth with a silly, open face.

What was Günther to him? His name and his face meant nothing to him; someone met by chance. Like that young Thimme, for instance.

Was he fond of Günther? Was he fond of anyone? Yes, he loved his race. He lived in the service of his race. Suppose Günther were not telling the truth? Or only half the truth? Suppose he were a traitor? In touch with the communists? Betraying the organisation?

Here Theodor was on to something. He must be careful. This something pointed a way.

Detective Klitsche heard Theodor out. Could not something more concrete be discovered?

There was nothing. Neither Günther's fiancée nor Günther himself gave anything away. Once, Theodor cautiously asked Günther if his future father-in-law were not a communist.

'Yes!' Günther laughed.

They wandered through the evening, arm in arm. Theodor and Günther. Power had numbed Theodor already, the mighty Theodor; already his fingers were tying the fatal noose of hate. Theodor, clever Theodor, saw his duty done, saw himself promoted over Klitsche, over Trebitsch, over everyone. He saw himself in Munich, a man of power, taking over the leadership. Theodor, a Führer. Swiftly, he went to Trebitsch and told him of Günther's treachery. He saw dangers, described them, stirred things up enthusiastically, encouraged by the approving smile of his bearded friend. That evening, Klitsche sent messages out; sixteen members of Branch S II met together, Trebitsch lit two candles and read through the Protocol with Theodor.

Had Günther admitted that his prospective father-in-law was a communist and head of a secret organisation?

Yes!

Had he armed the workers?

Yes!

And Günther was helping with this task?

Yes!

Paragraphs eight and nine of the Statutes ran as follows: 'Anyone taking action against the patriotic organisations, whether by stealth or main force, is condemned to death by summary justice. Likewise anyone having dealings with parties of the left without the knowledge of the leaders, other than for purposes of espionage.'

The student Günther is guilty.

Lots to be drawn?

'I'll take this one,' said Klitsche.

Silence. A sigh of astonished admiration reaches Klitsche. They sing a battle song:

> 'Let the traitors pay with blood,
> Slaughter them, this Jewish brood.
> *Deutschland über alles!*'

7

A gym practice was held at Weissensee, under the orders of Lieutenant Wachtl. A hundred paces away from everyone else walked Klitsche, Theodor and Günther. Günther had been invited as a guest, had been warmly greeted and entertained with jokes. Klitsche's loud laughter could be heard. They came to a halt and decided to have a rest. A woodpecker was drilling relentlessly, a bird called shyly. Hundreds of midges were dancing in the unseasonably warm April air, the earth in the woods smelt fresh and relaxing.

Theodor would be glad to see the end of the woods. But, oh, the woods have no end! Theodor is feverish, and the top of his skull feels as if the weight of many, many trees were pressing on it. Tears are forcing their way from his eyes so that he can no longer see. He slumps down beside Günther.

He is waiting now, waiting as if for his own death. It came too soon, too soon. Theodor saw countless tree trunks before his eyes, breaking and dimming the sunlight. But the trees were disembodied, ghost trees which would not stand still but were in constant, scarcely noticeable movement, as if the whole wood were an avenue, seen through a haze and moving in a gentle wind. More clearly than the tree trunks before him, Theodor sensed Detective Klitsche behind him; saw how he lifted a pickaxe with both hands and drew himself up, how he drew in his breath; and then Theodor closed his eyes. When he opened them again, he saw Günther collapsing at his side, saw the half-open mouth of the man lying on the ground, heard the half-choked cry which died in his throat, and sensed the overpowering silence. The woods were as still as if everything were waiting for the death cry which did not come.

Just at the bridge of Günther's nose, between his brows, stood the axe. His face was white, violet shadows beneath his eyes. He was still breathing. The thumb of his left hand, which lay across his chest, twitched like a little, dying pendulum of flesh. With a final gasp he drew back his upper lip, so one could see his teeth and a line of grey-white gum.

Klitsche threw a sack over Günther, leaving the pickaxe where it had struck. He hauled him over the pine-needles, across the sandy ground, over pinecones which crackled softly. There lay a pit, and into it he tumbled Günther.

Klitsche pulled off the sack so as to withdraw the axe. The blood spurted thick and red from Günther's forehead and fell with a soft, unceasing patter among the trees, a scarlet thread dripping from the pines.

They were sticky drops, which hardened at once, even as they fell. They formed a crust, like sealing-wax. An infinite frenzy of red surrounded Theodor. He had seen and heard this red in the war, it roared and screamed as if from a thousand throats, it flared and flickered like a thousand furnaces. The trees were red, the yellow sand and the pine-needles on the ground were red, red was the sky, so sharply outlined between the trunks of the pines, and the sunshine falling between the trees was a brilliant scarlet. Great purple wheels spun in the air, purple balls rolled up and down, glowing sparks danced in and out and transformed themselves into softly coiling snakes of fire before dispersing again. This frenzy of red came from within Theodor, filling him, bursting out of him, making him feel weightless, so that his head seemed to float, as if it were filled with air. It was like a weightless, crimson jubilation, a triumph which lifted him up in a floating frenzy which was death to his gloomy thoughts, and liberation for his soul which had been buried and concealed.

Klitsche slid sideways, fell, groaned once. The pickaxe stood upright for a while, pointing stiffly skywards, as if it were alive, then fell sideways. Theodor picked it up. He repeated Klitsche's action, lifted it high and smashed it down. Klitsche's skull cracked a little. Blood and brains flowed from his scalp. Somewhere or other, the woodpecker hammered indefatigably, the shy bird twittered and the heavy mist rose from the floor of the forest.

Theodor strode briskly through the trees, brittle twigs cracking under his feet, feeling as light as the countless dancing midges.

8

It was reported to Munich that Günther had struck down Klitsche and had afterwards been killed by Theodor Lohse. This was witnessed by the sixteen members of Section S II. The dead were properly buried. A squirrel, which had been shot and dismembered, lay on their grave and accounted for any traces of blood.

Theodor Lohse's way was clear. He took over and administered Klitsche's empire, and built it up. Hot was his breath, short was his sleep, and broad was the field that he tilled. He formed a guard, drawn from forty secondary schools. He disposed of unreliable spies. He lectured three times a week, preparing himself for half an hour beforehand. He drew on Trebitsch's essays and on the *Nationale Beobachter*. He disposed of the money which he received from Major Pauli. He wrote out accounts and distributed no advances except to himself.

He gradually understood connections which he had previously only divined from articles. He went to Munich and made the acquaintance of his immediate superior, a general who never went to Prussia and lived in Bavaria under the name of Major Seyfarth. He tried to call on Ludendorff, but was not allowed to, direct access to Ludendorff being forbidden. He lost his respect for certain men whom he had once thought and called great. He talked with National

Socialists and formed a low opinion of them because he discovered that they were not party to everything, and that secrets were not revealed to them either. Theodor learned to listen and doubt. People lied to him.

This hurt his feelings. People told him to stop asking questions. This sharpened his ambition and gave him fresh courage. He wanted influence, not merely independence. He wanted to be the first in line, not an invisible link. But his eagerness overwhelmed him, poured out of him, betrayed him, people distrusted his energy, and his zeal made him suspect. All of the generals, majors, bosses, students, journalists and politicians clung to their little positions and were ruled by anxiety about their daily bread; no more, no less. Among them little people came and went, guests of the organisation, the wandering speaker Schley, the pastor Blok who seduced schoolgirls, the student Biertimpfl, who had robbed a poor relief account, the artist Conti from Trieste, formerly a sailor and a deserter, the Jewish spy Baum whose speciality was troop deployment, the Alsatian Blum, a French agent, Klatko from Upper Silesia, invalided after the plebiscite battles; naval lieutenants, foreign Germans, fugitives from the occupied territories, cashiered privy councillors, prostitutes from Koblenz, street beggars from the Rhineland cities, Hungarian officers bringing unverifiable demands from Budapest from colleagues on the run and in search of forged passports, nameless editors looking for money with which to start short-lived newspapers. All of them knew something, were potentially dangerous and had to be fobbed off.

There were witty people and stupid people, from all of whom Theodor was able to learn, and others who tried to learn from him. Many people knew him, his name was familiar to them, and he had to watch out for spies. He had to watch out generally. He would walk through the streets with his hand on the butt of the revolver in his pocket. He avoided poorly-lit neighbourhoods, never stepped out of the house without carefully looking around, he sensed an enemy in every passer-by, and in every man who shared his way of thinking he sensed a rival. He could rely only on his group of young people. He formed a guard to deal with indoor and outdoor gatherings, broke up socialist meetings, marched through the streets singing lively songs. At Trebitsch's lectures he placed his people about the hall to applaud and encourage others to applaud. Sometimes an unsuspecting spectator would shout an insult. Theodor would then blow his whistle and the guards would come at the heckler from all sides, thrash him, knock him down, trample on his back, chest, skull and pitch into him with deadly delight.

He instructed, equipped, punished cowards and praised the courageous. A little god was he. He had excelled himself. His faith was long since shattered, his hatred diminished, his enthusiasm cooled off. He believed only in himself, loved only himself and was enchanted only by his own doings. He no longer hated the Efrussis, nor did he hate the Glasers. He did not believe that the movement would succeed. He began to see through Trebitsch. He could see the senselessness of the catch phrases and the beliefs. He despised the audiences which he addressed. He knew that they swallowed everything. He read pamphlets and newspapers, not so as to pass on their meaning but to learn them by heart and to store in his head convictions to which he was perfectly indifferent. He observed that everyone worked for himself alone, but he worked harder than the others. He wanted . . . He himself was not sure what he wanted.

He wanted to be a leader, a member of the Bundestag, a Minister, a dictator. He was still unknown outside his own circle. The name Theodor Lohse did not make banner headlines in the papers. He would gladly have been a martyr for fame, and have sacrificed his life to the popularity of his name. It hurt him that all his activities must remain anonymous. And as the strength of his convictions diminished, so he widened the scope of his artificial hatreds: he now spoke not only against the workers and the Jews and the French, but also against the Catholics, those Romans. His gang raided the hall in which the Catholic writer, Lambrecht, was speaking. Theodor sat in the front row. Over his head flew sentences from some alien, incomprehensible language. But one word registered, the word 'Talmud'. It impinged on Theodor's half-dormant conscience. He whistled, and forty large members of his mob dived into the audience. Theodor screamed: 'Jew! Roman!' at Lambrecht. He formed a great oyster of spittle on his tongue and launched it at Lambrecht. He hauled a grey-haired woman by her hair along the rows of seats, twisting her wrists. The woman kicked him, yelled at him. Suddenly she grew heavy and fell. The whistle sounded. Everyone disappeared. The police found only a *fait accompli* and arrested two of the injured in whose pockets they had found red buttons and who turned out to be harmless members of a bowling club.

Theodor loved Franziska, a spy, who had come to him. She brought him information about the Communist Party, her hair was cut short, her skin *café-au-lait*. He wept when she disappeared with his cash-box and his reports, and he was short of money. The postman Janitschke claimed payment for letters he had stolen. He had a withered arm but waved the other threateningly. His spy, Braune, wanted the fare to Frankfurt, his wife had had a child and he must go home.

Theodor reported the Franziska episode and had to make good the money himself; he asked Trebitsch for help. Trebitsch suggested he try Efrussi.

He waited for a long time in the anteroom. He had waited the same long time when he had first come to Efrussi, looking for a job as a tutor. The bell rang, twice, three times, the servant in his dark suit moved stiffly, his chest thrust out, his knees straight, like a wooden man. Efrussi's face was still the pale, cold, suffering face of an old, strict woman, and in his presence one became a tutor, a bygone Theodor Lohse, a rather little Theodor Lohse.

Efrussi asked for a receipt. He put the cheque into an envelope and said: 'Go to Major Pauli.' He gave the order, Theodor obeyed it, he went to Major Pauli, he understood, he knew. Efrussi's power was great, he was stronger than any Theodor Lohse, one never ceased to be his house tutor, his servant, his dependant. And the old hatred awoke in Theodor, screamed inside him: blood, blood, Jews' blood!

Only as he stood before Major Pauli did he draw himself from slump to attention, and lose his dispirited look. Melancholy became respect, and with swift determination he mustered all his strength for one purpose only: to hold himself like a soldier. The voice of the major swept away the painful memory of his begging visit to Efrussi, and the echo of his heels snapping together rang in his ears as he left and returned to his work room. No more adventures threatened him. Messengers came, and letters, which he slit open with the flat paper-knife whose cool ivory surface he loved to caress.

9

From time to time the late Klitsche's brother turned up. He was serving in the *Reichswehr*. While speaking he stood fiercely to attention, and fifteen times a minute he said '*Herr Leutnant*'. And yet somehow he seemed to fit in with all the things in this room. His eye took in the carpets, the covers, the floorboards as old acquaintances. He had lain on this sofa, sat on that chair, and he looked like the Klitsche who was dead. So like him that Theodor could neither forget the face of the dead man, nor the reason why he himself was actually sitting here, working, working, growing.

Had this brother of Klitsche's not existed, Theodor would have eased up – and although he couldn't be absolutely sure of it, he probably would have rested. He sometimes longed for a break. But then Klitsche's face would surface, or Günther's, and Theodor worked. He had killed them both, and not in vain. It had been his duty to report the one and, as for the other, he was perhaps already dead before the killing madness overcame Theodor, and this had been a task which had borne fruit.

There were, however, evenings when Theodor was compelled to consider the question of whether the dead are dead for good and all. Then he would go to the Kaiser-Wilhelm, the little bar where he was known, where they said 'Good day, *Herr Leutnant*,' and valued his custom. One or two companions from his group would butter him up and move over to make room for him in the middle, would study his mouth and, if they deduced from his first remarks that the stories would be funny, they laughed and were overwhelmed by Theodor's humour. Theodor knew many stories, he was the hero and the cynosure of all eyes: not for nothing had he been a regular and laughed there for years; he knew now that the one who told the stories was the centre of attraction. Sometimes, too, he would forget and think the stories were about himself. For he drank, and the applause set the wind in his tail so that he would sit astride the high bar stool and feel as if he were galloping.

From a great distance he could hear his friends' laughter, the music which was being played in the big room and which had been inaudible now drew nearer, they were playing the song of the nut-brown maid, and it was so sad that Theodor was almost in tears and wondered why the barmaid was smiling.

He drank another cocktail, sank from his stool and woke up next day.

How gladly he would have yielded to a different kind of relaxation! It was lovely to roam in the open air, summer lay broad and powerful across the land, and in the woods there were . . . Theodor was not happy in the woods. The dead lay in the woods, they were eaten by worms and green grass grew from their limbs.

Rest came later, one only found it on the heights, the road was long and Theodor was tired.

But something drove him towards the heights, unseen, unknown, scarcely imaginable. Within him and about him, something cried: upwards. He knew the way now, now he was a *Gruppenführer*, now he was on good terms with the journalists, knew the politician Hilper, went to the Reichstag gallery. He could picture himself speaking, he saw himself in this great hall at the head of his men, could hear his shrill whistle. He would strike down the members, drive them out and cry: 'Long live the dictatorship!' Up above, high up, beside the dictator, stood Theodor.

He recalled his old method: he made direct contact with the high up and the highest. He knew them now. Beyond his 'Major Seyfarth' stood the naval captain, 'Hartmut'. Theodor made plans: he studied the lives and the habits of Jews and socialists; he found out a lot and made up the rest. He wrote in the *Nationale Beobachter* about a connection he had discovered between a politician and French agents, and obliquely recommended an assassination. He cunningly found supporting evidence for every accusation. He exaggerated facts and manipulated them, while every event attracted his suspicion. Occasionally he would sniff out a secret connection. Journalists would draw his attention to improbable coincidences. He sent his spies out. He knew that every spy exaggerated and he would embroider their exaggerations. He invented plans for rescuing imprisoned members of the organisation. He sent the plans to Munich – to Captain Hartmut. He made money, if nothing else. He drew expenses. He would appease disgruntled spies with a comradely handclasp. There were dumb ones who went along with it. They waited.

But Section S, 'Major Seyfarth', sent reproofs and warnings, and summoned Theodor to Munich. Theodor would talk his way out. He went from 'Major Seyfarth' to 'Captain Hartmut', who was an old gentleman with thin hair combed forward over a bald head, who listened gratefully and insatiably to compliments and flattery. Theodor had his measure. From time to time he would let fall a cautious comment on the subject of Section S, but as for the Captain –

that would be another matter. He needed a free spirit, did Theodor Lohse.

He was forgetting that Trebitsch existed, that Trebitsch had to earn his keep; that he, too, had to prepare accounts; that it was his duty to keep an eye on Theodor. And Trebitsch reported that in his enthusiasm Theodor had exaggerated in this case and drawn a false conclusion in that. Oh, yes, the Jew Trebitsch had reliable eyes and ears.

Theodor was preparing to rescue a man imprisoned awaiting trial. He went to Leipzig. One of the guards had been a sergeant in Theodor's company. He wanted to win him over for the organisation. He reported good progress to Munich. And he received a visit from a man who bore orders in writing to proceed that very day, or at the latest the next, to the Luschka Estate in Pomerania, with fifty men.

10

He was powerless, embittered, vengeful. He went to Trebitsch . . . Was not Theodor Lohse indispensable?

And Trebitsch smiled. He ran his outspread fingers through his beard. There was nothing he could do; Theodor set off.

The farm labourers on the Luschka Estate had gone on strike. The Freiherr von Kockwitz was calling for help.

He was old, the Freiherr von Kockwitz, and a widower. He had three sons: Friedrich, Kurt and Wilhelm. He was a hunter. A crack shot. He shot all day long. He had an arsenal of weapons in his basement. He was strict with himself and others. He received Theodor at about noon. The sun was blazing. Theodor's men had an hour's march behind them. The Freiherr demanded military order of march. Were these men tramps? Did they wander about in straggling groups? He demanded that they form fours. He pointed the way to the great barn, a quarter of an hour away. Theodor marched in bitterness, powerless, thirsting for vengeance. He knew the Freiherr von Kockwitz.

Everybody knew him. He had once shot a labourer during tree felling. He threatened Sunday excursionists with loaded weapons. In his woods children disappeared looking for wild strawberries. In summer his sons hid behind hedges, ambushing picnickers, shooting at the *Wandervogel*. The youngest son was twelve and picked off the forester's doves. Irritation with Freiherr von Kockwitz had driven his wife into an early grave. Her maiden name had been von Zick. Her grandfather was known to have been in the postal service, a young aristocrat of the mail coaches. The newspapers wrote about the Freiherr von Kockwitz. The law courts allowed indictments to wither away. Public prosecutors were invited to shoot on his estate. Investigating magistrates played poker with him. People knew about the Freiherr von Kockwitz. They hated him. They would tell Kockwitz anecdotes. Every year his labourers went on strike. Every year, the people from Rossbach had to help him out. People feared this summer work. One ate twice a day when one worked for the Freiherr von Kockwitz; barley soup and black bread.

The men lay in the barn, angry and hungry. The Freiherr von Kockwitz appeared and gave orders: 'Have your people sing! I love singing!' They sang, they worked, they ate barley soup and black bread, they went to sleep, and rose at the first gleam of daylight. They sang. Once, the Freiherr came into the fields. He was in a good mood. He had invited the magistrate. He talked to Theodor, grumbled about his striking labourers. Bunch of Polacks. Not a drop of German blood. They were being corrupted by Jews. In this part of the world there was nothing but Jews and Polacks, a rabble of reds. They needed suppressing and suppressed they would be. That night the great barn caught fire. One of Theodor's people had been smoking. The Freiherr threatened three days' stoppage of pay, but the magistrate suspected the striking labourers. Ten were imprisoned. The next day a hundred of them appeared in front of the house. The Freiherr had machine pistols brought up from the cellars. He lost his appetite, closed the shutters, boxed twelve-year-old Wilhelm's ears. He already saw his house in ruins. His sons hanged. Himself on the rack. He gave up going into the fields. He slept in his clothes, with his pistol by his side. He was afraid of poisoned food. He was just afraid.

Theodor slept in the house. Not just because the barn had burned down. Theodor organised watches. His men stood guard. The old man grew gentle, a kind old greybeard. He gave money to the church. He looked about him when he spoke. He whispered.

In this mood he was open to any suggestion.

Theodor was embittered. So they wanted to be rid of him? They wanted his name to disappear? The name of Theodor Lohse was going to blaze from every newspaper. People were not going to forget Theodor Lohse. Not in Berlin, not in Munich. People would not forget him.

One must challenge these labourers. If it came to a fight, annihilate them. A hundred men. Did they have weapons? There was an arsenal here. People would not forget Theodor Lohse. Every day, they sang:

The traitor pays with blood,
Shoot them down, the Jewish brood!
Deutschland über alles . . .

The men did less work. They drilled. They went out with their weapons. The labourers were starving. Their children were developing thin necks and big heads. The women hissed when they saw Theodor's men. They shouted: 'Dogs!'

Theodor's men fired in the air. Labourers appeared on all sides, a hundred, two hundred. They carried sticks and threw stones. They came towards the house.

Theodor let them into the courtyard. Once in, they started shouting. They pushed against the walls, window panes tinkled pathetically. Inside the windows hung mattresses to catch the stones. A worker, carried on the shoulders of his comrades, was urging them on. Theodor fired. The worker reeled. They broke in all directions. They regrouped at the gate and wrestled in vain with the triple lock. They struggled over the walls, but on the other side rifles were blazing. The workers let themselves drop into the courtyard. From the house shots echoed.

The dying groaned. The living made no sound. A great stillness spread. Silence drifted over the courtyard as if from a broad, open grave. The paving stones reflected the hot sun. High up in the air, larks were trilling. A bumblebee hummed like a great top. From far away came a dog's bark. The church bell in the village sounded.

Many escaped over the walls, pushed aside the threatening weapons and fled. Thirty dead and wounded remained. Trickles of blood drew maps on the white stones of the courtyard.

The police arrived later and drank beer in the courtyard. The blood hadn't dried. The young magistrate had a dimple in his childish chin and a swastika pin in his buttonhole.

The newspapers wrote: 'Bloody Uprising of Farmworkers. Heroic Action by the Voluntary Service Men!' The world took notice. Reporters came. Theodor Lohse spoke with them. Theodor Lohse was in the papers. A student, a lieutenant in the Reserve, had beaten back the uprising: Theodor Lohse.

That Sunday was a flag day for the voluntary services. On the streets of Berlin, white-clothed children were selling linen cornflowers.

11

Theodor heard his red blood shouting as if from a thousand throats, he saw the flames of a thousand fires, great purple wheels spun in the air, purple balls rose and fell. The overwhelming redness came from within him, it filled him and made him light. A crimson jubilation possessed him, he was uplifted in triumph.

But during the hours of evening, when the bats began to flit and the frogs to croak, when the ceaseless song of the crickets became more persistent and some maid sang as she finished her work for the day, he would grow melancholy. Touched, and tearful of soul, he would look at the red sky of evening and whistle sad tunes to himself. It was like being in the Kaiser-Wilhelm when the band played the song of the nut-brown maid.

He would recover his faith in the cause he served when the old Freiherr grew sad and began to talk of German land now fallen into the hands of the Polacks. Somewhere, Theodor heard the call of the hunting horns and the fearsome, cold and mortal summons of the battle trumpet. He was back in the midst of war and ready to sacrifice his blood if the old Freiherr gave the word: Homeland. He would fight and struggle to defend its sacred earth. The Freiherr used a long, nostalgic O and a hard, East Prussian L. He would draw in his breath before uttering the first syllable, and then release it on the second, with a sigh. Theodor often saw in the old gentleman the image of one of the last German noblemen, threatened with extinction by the new times.

It was not always like this. When it was raining and Theodor sat in the Freiherr's library, he would read the novels in *Die Woche* and study photographs of great men in the newspapers. Then he would become timid, as he always had been, and the old gentleman would lose his magic and just seem an eccentric old man, as everyone else regarded him. He understood and excused him, however, and was grateful to him for his exceptionally generous and enjoyable hospitality.

For Theodor was living better than any previous voluntary service man. Theodor was a witness in the case against the farm labourers. He conferred with the magistrate. He accompanied the Freiherr to Berlin. It was already clear that no risk whatever was involved. Moreover, Theodor was treated well. A badly wounded worker, who was being held under suspicion of being the ringleader, rapidly recovered in hospital. They even gave him wine, once his temperature had dropped. The charges against him went from housebreaking and breach of the peace to material damage and attempted murder.

The case took half an hour. The labourer was given eight months' imprisonment. That evening, the Public Prosecutor sat with Theodor Lohse over a bottle of wine in the Kaiserhof.

A week later, Theodor took his leave of the estate. He could not disguise the depth of his feeling. He thought of how the old Freiherr would soon be dead, he thought of the evenings and the sound of frogs and crickets, the dangers which had united him with the house, and to the sacred Homeland.

He then marched off, at the head of his fifty men, to the station. They sang along the broad highway. Theodor decided not to pay them until they reached Berlin. At the moment of departure, the Freiherr had not withheld the three days' pay.

But Theodor thought of doing so.

12

He went to see Trebitsch. His greeting was triumphant. Did they think he was dead? Look, Theodor was alive! More alive than ever. Had they forgotten him? His name stared out of the papers.

He shed his melancholy, forgot the song of the crickets, the song of the maids, the Homeland. He got back to work at once. He went to Leipzig. But the prisoner Pfeifer had flown without his help. Trebitsch had had him set free.

Theodor was stung by the missed opportunity. But Zange and Martinelli were still being held.

He went to Munich. He found Captain Hartmut distrustful. Trebitsch had been at work. He recognised his touch.

National Socialism was a phrase like any other. It required no definition. He was received with respect by the National Socialist leaders, before others, who were kept waiting. So they knew him, but they did not know *about* him. Theodor delicately drew aside a veil or two, to arouse their curiosity. They lived in a whirl of enthusiasm. People were flocking to join them. They were a Party, not a secret society. That seemed more powerful to Theodor. In a Party one worked with one's visor open, not buried underground. In a Party, one's name rang like a thousand bells.

He went to meetings. Everyone was jubilant. Little citizens drank beer; ate and cheered with their mouths full of cabbage and pigs' knuckles. Young storm troopers marched into the hall, lined the walls, carried the speaker along a lane cleared between the chairs, the public, and the tables. Four thousand feet were stamping. White-coated waiters darted. Banknotes rustled. It was a people's celebration. Theodor was envious.

And his work was slinking about undercover, spied on by enemies from within and without?

He went to the recruiting offices. How they poured in! Young labourers, students, office workers. Different material from Theodor's schoolboys. They were more trusting, more easily worked on, afire before they came and white-hot if they were accepted. Hitler was a menace. Was Theodor Lohse a menace? The newspapers spoke of Hitler every day. When did one see Theodor's name?

But these big, naive, uneducated men, living in a whirl of enthusiasm, needed taming. Men with so little knowledge were sufficient to themselves. They knew nothing about discussion. It was not necessary to them. When the Führer left his office, fifty men in the anteroom saluted him and twenty stood to attention. He drove in his car. It was possible that he was not aware of everything, that he was a pawn. But everybody knew him, and who noticed Theodor Lohse?

Major Seyfarth was displeased. How would he get round him? Theodor recalled his services. Theodor threatened. The major leaped to his feet. Had Theodor not sworn the oath? An oath can be broken. Theodor Lohse's power was based on two hundred bold men. Theodor exaggerated. A bare fifty schoolboys followed him. They were young and timid.

Seyfarth backed off. He had a solution. Was there not enough work for Theodor Lohse? Agitation? Propaganda? In the *Reichswehr*, perhaps? Was that not a solution? One made valuable contacts.

Theodor thought it over: the two hundred men had impressed him! Now he was afraid of them. The army promised well. Would his pay continue? Yes, and he would also get his army pay on top of it. He volunteered.

At home, he looked in the mirror. He looked no different from that Führer. Nobody pushed him around. He flashed a smile at his reflection. Uttered a word to test his voice. His voice carried. It could thunder.

He made a plan for the *Reichswehr*: he must find devoted people, become their teacher, their leader, master of life and death for a hundred, two hundred, a thousand armed men.

He joined up. The formalities only took a day. He joined with five references. Potsdam was his garrison. He wore a uniform of the latest cut. The coat was no longer close-fitting, as it had been in the old days. This was in the new spirit of the army. The silver stripes on the epaulettes were now so positioned as to reveal a narrow border of cloth. The bayonet joint was thinly nickeled. Its use was no longer outlined in the exercise manuals, but it was still good-humouredly tolerated. He drilled every morning. It was a long time since he had done so. He stood before two ranks of men. He noted the slightest variation between one body and another. He saw when someone moved, when boots had not been polished, rifles had not been oiled, packs had been put on crooked. He would order 'Knees bend!' and he was obeyed, 'At the double!' and they doubled, 'Halt!' and they halted.

In the afternoon he would give instruction. He would read from Trebitsch's pamphlets. And he said his own piece. He would make a joke. The soldiers would laugh. He thought he noticed that one was not well. He sent him home. He was a comrade. He would clap one or another on the shoulder. He talked about girls. On Mondays he would ask how Sunday had been. On Saturdays he would wish them a pleasant Sunday. He would put a good word in with the colonel on behalf of the men under punishment. He himself avoided awarding punishment and made do with reprimands. He gathered round him the men who had seen action.

He would announce lectures for the evenings. Many came. His company approved, and brought others with them. After a few weeks he was able to speak his mind. He asked how many of them would go through thick and thin with him. They all stood up, every one of them. He made one or two of them swear an oath. He gave these money, and pamphlets to distribute.

He talked little with the officers. He went into the mess. Like everyone else, they talked about the dollar. Lieutenant Schutz, son of a senior banker, had sold stocks to the colonel. There was a bull market. The colonel's good humour made the mess cheerful. They all wanted to invest, they knew what securities were, and a rising market, and margins. Lieutenant Schutz lent them all money. He also lent money to Theodor.

Theodor read the market prices in the evening papers.

13

He studied the stock prices.

His money increased: he learnt to call it capital growth. Now the road was open. The road to those shining white villas in the Tiergarten, standing among silky green lawns, behind silvery railings, with their stiff footmen and the pictures in gilt frames. Theodor had forgotten almost everything else about them. Mightiest of all was Efrussi. One never ceased to be his house tutor. Capital growth led towards the secrets of power.

He, Theodor Lohse, had always loved money. He had brought off his first coup at school. He had taken a collection for a wreath. Young Berger had died. He took two marks forty, bought the wreath for two marks ten and pocketed the thirty pfennigs. He had kept them for a whole year.

He had always been a saver. As a student, and later in the army, he had learned to appreciate the value of money. Only with Trebitsch's first cheques had he been extravagant. He had regretted it later. He always regretted having spent it.

He travelled in civilian clothes, and third class. He bought season tickets for the suburban train. In uniform, he would go on foot.

Early in the day, when they were doubling round the fields, exercising, he would see the sweet-seller surrounded by soldiers. She was selling lemonade. They were all hot and drinking it. Theodor would bite on some chewing-gum.

He smoked three times a day, after each meal. A single cigar was enough for him. He would put it out and light it again.

He watched his money growing. When he was as rich as Efrussi, he would buy himself a Theodor Lohse.

In the meantime he stood in front of the shop windows and calculated what he could buy if he were to sell his holdings. From time to time he would enquire of door-to-door salesmen how much this or that house cost. He received much information of this kind, and divided the houses into those he could not afford and those for which he had enough money.

All this almost made him forgetful of his duties. He was like a bridegroom who oversleeps on his wedding morning. His observant eye was straying to distant fields. His slumbering ears no longer marked the approaching thunder of the times. He no longer saw Trebitsch, no longer wrote for the *Nationale Beobachter*.

He walked indifferently past the food shops, in front of which hungry crowds raised their voices. One afternoon, workmen went looting in Potsdam.

The barracks were quietly busy. A strange machine-gun company reported for duty – no one knew for how long. No one knew the *Oberleutnant* in command.

People were less talkative. The colonel sat stiff and silent. His cheeks were dark-red-and-blue-veined. When he was not talking, they hung like little bags of skin over his collar. At the foot of the mess table, where the 'young people' sat, no one joked any more. People read the political pages of the newspapers and ceased to concern themselves with money.

It was a time of anxious solemnity, as if people were expecting some catastrophe to bring them a happy release. Major von Lubbe delivered a lecture on the future of aerial warfare. It was a well-known lecture, which Major von Lubbe was wont to read once a year out of the *Kreuzzeitung*.

As a captain, he had composed an article on aerial warfare. That was a long time ago. When he read his lecture, the staff officers would withdraw. Only the junior officers had to stay and listen. The major talked about Count Zeppelin. He had once been invited to Count Zeppelin's. And in fact the lecture dealt less with aerial warfare than with the personality of the Count.

On this occasion the staff officers did not withdraw. It was not appropriate in the circumstances, which required the strictest observance of military and social etiquette. But on this occasion the major did not have so much to say about Count Zeppelin. He spoke of the Count's times, comparing them with the present day and extolling German unity. And he spoke of imminent tasks. And even the staff officers listened.

In two weeks' time the dedication of a memorial was to take place. The regiment had invited all its former officers, and also General Ludendorff. Naturally, he would come. The colonel announced it in the mess; he spoke slowly, visibly shaping each syllable, and his jaws worked so hard that his dewlaps trembled.

They drilled with renewed energy. Rifles were cleaned, barrels oiled, arms drill practised. The band practised, polishing up old marches.

And the people in the towns went hungry. News of a general strike flared in the newspapers. The workers shuffled heavily and slowly through the streets in the evenings. Their women waited. The men did not come home. The hearth was cold and there was no food ready. What would they do at home? They went into the drink shops. There was enough money for schnaps, and the drunk feel no hunger. The drunks lurched and dragged their feet along the asphalt. Streets were sealed off. Police helmets sprang up. Roller-curtains hung like iron coffin lids over shattered shop windows. The shots which were not fired awaited their hour of blood.

A confidential order reached Theodor. Triple attention to duty. To Theodor this was a clarion call. His time was coming. He was prepared. He was armed for the day. It could be today or tomorrow.

He summoned his guard. The young people came. They brought fresh comrades from the *Bismarck-Bund*. They brought pistols for the shoot-out. Theodor went to the master-at-arms. All weapons were cleaned. Old bayonets gleamed. The youngsters spent a day in barracks. How the rusty old weapons exhilarated them! And how the shiny new ones dazzled them! How could they know about them? This rifle or that had been through all the wars. It had killed the enemy. A rifle butt gave off great power, and the pommel of a sabre was a thing of magic. What gallant horsemen had wielded it? The steel was dull ... from blood, said some! Patches of rust were bloodstains. The blood of the enemy clinging to the steel.

The general came on Sunday.

On Sunday, the regiment marched out, band playing. The October sun shone as if it were spring. People waved from their windows. Flags fluttered. Children ran beside them. It was like peacetime. Many forgot their poverty.

They stood before the general. The old divisional chaplain addressed them. The spike on Ludendorff's helmet blazed in the sun. A soft tinkle of medals came from the officers, a silvery, faint music. Spurs jingled like bells. The soldiers' breath lay heavy on the air like some solemn ceremonial. One could hear the quiet voices of the officers from the middle of the square. A short, harsh laugh from the general, more of a gurgle.

The general spoke three sentences, from the right of the

memorial tablet. They were hard words. He clasped his hands over the pommel of his sword. One could have taken him for a statue, a statue in full dress uniform.

Then he stepped down, inserting his monocle whenever he spoke with anyone. He spoke to Theodor. Once I wrote him a letter, thinks Theodor. What a long time ago! How young Theodor was, even half a year ago! Today Ludendorff knows him.

14

Secret orders warned them to stand by for November 2nd. Theodor had three weeks' grace. He no longer slept. His days were filled with aimless haste. In the evening he would consider his pointless activity. Through the watches of the night one decision went round and round, but without a plan: he must become powerful. The speed with which things were happening was too great for him. He would have wasted his time if, on November 2nd, he were still only halfway there, not the leader. Just a link in the chain, not its beginning. One among many, not senior to them. In that case he could expect no distinction, only humble ambitions.

Into the circle of his worries, heroic dreams would explode, he would hear the drumbeat of his mission, and crimson jubilation would sweep him to the heights. Günther and Klitsche and eighteen workers were dead, a fruitless tally for eight months of enthusiasm. He had been a misused tool in other people's hands. And to what purpose? He would think nothing of it if he reached his goal; it would kill him if he failed.

He ought to restrain himself no longer, yet he had allowed himself time, at least a year, in which to go on spinning his web; people and things were still hidden from his eyes. He had been cast aside, his keenness had betrayed him. He should have chosen his way with greater care. He was now doing what hundreds of others were doing: giving lectures, distributing brochures. It was a long time since he had been to Munich . . . who was to know if there were not new leaders, and chance might yet bring some other Klitsche to the surface.

Just one more year — and he would be rich, and money would provide him with everything that hard work did not. But before him stood November 2nd. The nearness of the day confused him and prevented him from giving due consideration to his decisions. The earth quaked beneath him, his path no longer climbed upwards.

On half-days he travelled between Potsdam and Berlin. He would read the incoming mail in his office and then go to Trebitsch, that perfect example of a man quietly certain of his aims. Trebitsch behaved as if he were standing apart. He was of the same sort as those who were hammering out the words 'November 2nd', harmless and gentle. His spade beard lent him the appearance of a worthy and a harmless man, a man of ideas, an absent-minded professor. Only an inattentive phrase gave him away. He noticed everything, just as Theodor did when he faced his company. He spoke of the 'alternative method' of handling the workers. Perhaps, in the future, it would become a question of winning over the radical left. The watchwords now were: be careful; remain calm; no provocation.

Inside Theodor, hidden from the dangers of discovery, there still lay the old, ill-defined, carefully formed wish to throw a bridge over to those others. The ringing phrases of the oath had floated away, their fearfulness was dimmed, their threat devoid of force. What happened to a man of power? Danger still threatened him – until he reached those others. Was there not danger here? The others were easier to grasp. He sensed that they were men of honour. Here it was all self-seeking, worrying about money, job, wife and child. Over there lived the diviners of gold, the crucified, who spoke of the Good and of the New Testament.

There is not much danger now. There is always a door ajar. Today Theodor can make efforts independently. To whom must he account? Who suspects him? He can answer for everything. It must be obvious that he keeps projects secret, since their success depends on their secrecy. He can risk it.

What was socialism? A word. One is not bound to believe in it. What did he believe in today? Over there he was valued. The others opened their arms. He knew those corridors.

In the night watches his plan developed, came to life and drove forward to fulfilment. Theodor had no time left. He must think about the first steps.

Is he a traitor? He is not. In truth, he only wants to overhear the others, to keep a check on his spies. He must not think too long. Reflection weakens decision. There is no time.

Day after day the headlines flared above the news. Already the Saxon metalworkers were striking. People talked of trains being held up somewhere. In the barracks they came to the second state of readiness.

15

Among the unreliable and suspect spies whom Theodor had dismissed was Benjamin Lenz. He had made double reports: to Trebitsch and to Theodor. He had been paid by both of them. Theodor got in touch with him.

Lenz, a Jew from Lodz, had worked during the war as a spy for a news and espionage agency. His appearance betrayed him: his prominent cheekbones threw shadows onto his eyes, while the lower part of his forehead and his eyebrows protruded. His black little eyes lay, as it were, in a narrow ravine, guarded on all sides and making it difficult to judge in which direction they were looking because they were so deep-set. His chin was short but broad and his nose was flat. This head, which would have suited a heavily-built torso, was perched on a skinny neck between narrow, sloping shoulders. Benjamin Lenz had small bones, slender wrists and long, nervous fingers.

He had come back to Germany with the returning armies and had drifted through many towns. He had references from the army. Policemen, although they despised his type, beckoned Benjamin towards them with understanding in their eyes. They favoured him, and he cut his cloth to suit the times, played the tunes they wanted to hear, fed false news to foreign missions, stole documents and official stamps from government offices, went spying in Upper Silesia and had himself imprisoned in company with people under investigation, so that he could overhear them, while waiting for 'his day' to dawn.

The name of his god was: Benjamin Lenz. He hated Europe, Christianity, Jewry, Monarchy, Republics, Philosophy, Political Parties, Ideas and Nations. He served the Powers only so as to study their weakness, their malice, their cunning and their Achilles heels. He betrayed them more than he exploited them. He hated the stupidity of Europe. His cleverness hated it. He was cleverer than politicians, journalists and everyone else who had power or the means of access to power. He tried out his strength on them. He betrayed organisations to their political opponents; to the French Missions he conveyed a mixture of truth and falsehood. He took pleasure in the gullible faces of the people he betrayed, who would find in his corrupt intelligence the excuse to perpetrate fresh enormities. He took pleasure in the stupid astonishment of conceited diplomats, childish and powerless counsellors, bestial Nazis, and rejoiced that they did not see through him. He seldom made mistakes, but he was not aware that Klitsche was dead and that another ruled in his place. For this reason, a long and successfully executed manoeuvre with Trebitsch, discovered by Theodor, brought him under suspicion. He had been supplying Trebitsch with false material. But he had managed to get away with it. He acted the stupid little spy. He had to have his missions explained to him several times over. He refused anything complicated. He played the part of a man whose intelligence is just sufficient to grasp his own limitations.

And he waited.

On 'his day', all over Europe, the madness which was slumbering would explode. For this reason he encouraged chaos, incited bloodlust and self-destruction, betrayed one man to another and that other to a third. He made money. But he lived in one small room of a dirty hotel. He ate in furtive cellar restaurants, with beggars and robbers. He was saving up for his brother, his two sisters, his aged father. His father was an old army medical orderly with a little Jewish barber's shop in Lodz. His sisters needed dowries. His brother, who was studying chemistry, received the largest part of his earnings. It was planned that this brother would be able one day to open a factory of his own. Benjamin never went near him. He never wrote to his father in Lodz. Benjamin had no time; he was working towards his day.

Theodor had not dismissed him simply because of the double dealing. He could smell his cleverness. He sensed Benjamin's Jewishness. As a gun dog will scent game in any direction, so would Theodor sniff out a Jew if opportunity offered.

Lenz turned up half an hour late, leaving Theodor to wait. Anyone who needed him he kept waiting. And he refused to fulfil Theodor's wish. He always refused. Lead Theodor Lohse to those others? What about Comrade Trattner? They knew him, knew Theodor's portrait. Klaften had taken several sketches of him: to the life.

Theodor had buried that Klaften episode. He asked how it had worked out. 'Nothing came of it,' said Lenz. Thimme, the young conspirator, had been a police spy. Goldscheider was in hospital, Klaften was now a well-known painter. His portrait of Theodor had won a prize in some exhibition. After a quarter of an hour Benjamin Lenz no longer refused. Could he read people's minds? Everything could indeed be forgotten, said Lenz, if Theodor would come as a friend. Or seemingly as a friend.

They went.

16

There they sat, three men in a café on the Potsdamer Platz, exchanging small talk, distrust sticking in their gullets, their tongues slowed by anxiety. At a nearby table sat Benjamin Lenz.

Theodor regretted all this. It was too late. He had had no idea that it would prove so difficult. He had to make an opening. Nobody helped him. It was almost as if they were cultivating his misery.

And now it is as it once was – a long time ago – at school, when he had to say something which he had not learned by heart. The café was noisy, the hum of conversation came from the neighbouring tables, cups clinked, and yet a silence faced him, as if everyone were expectant. Only as they were walking through the streets did he recover his self-possession. He walked between two dark shadows who marked his every word.

He was not dissembling. Why should he dissemble? He could always deny things, make a frank admission instead of a trumped-up one. His true motives sounded convincing.

He described his dissatisfaction, the distrust which was all about him; admitted that he was driven by ambition.

Later, in an office, he could sense the iceberg tip of secrets.

It was late before he left, and he went to Potsdam, read an evening paper. He looked up, to see Benjamin Lenz. He was sitting facing him.

They walked through the Potsdam evening, along the old lanes which looked quite unreal, and Benjamin led the way and Theodor was unaware of being led. Benjamin Lenz spoke of November 2nd. He did not believe in revolutions. He believed there would be a small bloodbath, hardly worth worrying about, of the kind which was quite liable to happen at times in Germany; any old week, in fact.

Perhaps Benjamin was saying what he really meant, this time?

It was a nostalgic evening, the clouds reflected in violet and yellow, the evening breeze gentle and consoling, and Theodor walked beneath the rustling trees and along the road which led to the station, feeling moved in the way that he had felt during those days in the fields of the Freiherr von Kockwitz.

A warmth emanated from Benjamin Lenz, so that Theodor began to talk and ceased to weigh his words and complained of Trebitsch and of ingratitude in general. What was a man of Lohse's ability doing in the *Reichswehr*?

What was a man of his kind doing in the *Reichswehr*? came Benjamin Lenz's heartening echo. Who had thwarted him? It was a question of finding out, for one must know one's opponent.

Oh yes, how well Lenz knew it. One should keep on good terms with Benjamin Lenz.

How much did he not know, even about Theodor? He knew it all. Did he also have his suspicions about the Klitsche episode? He knew all about it. He said: 'You cannot have shed blood for no reason, Lieutenant Lohse. Others can wade through corpses because of an idea, or because they are born murderers. But you, Herr Lohse, have not believed in the idea for a long time, and you are no born murderer. You are no politician, either. You were overtaken by your profession. You did not choose it. You were not satisfied with your life, your income and your social status. You should have tried to demand more from life within the framework of your own personality, rather than choosing a life which runs contrary to your gifts and to your temperament.'

No, Theodor could not and should not have acted differently. He could have remained small and unnoticed had he not changed roads, he could have stayed on as tutor with the Efrussis, and contentedly.

On this nostalgic evening, he thought of Frau Efrussi. The soft pressure of her upper arm in the car, her smile.

The road, at the end of which power was waiting, also led to her and others of her kind. How openly he spoke, this spy, Benjamin. There are evenings, thought Theodor, when people must perforce be good, as if under a spell.

Then Günther came into his mind, Günther who had loved his fiancée; he saw his face, and the mauve tint beneath his eyes, the exposed upper jaw, the painfully snarling lips.

How sadly trains hooted in the night. Peace came from a blue sky.

Benjamin Lenz walks beside Theodor, and is perhaps his friend.

He is your companion in arms, Theodor. His cunning is useful. Two heads together will succeed. And who but Lenz can be your ally? Benjamin Lenz understands Theodor Lohse.

They walked the long way back: between them fell the soothing silence of friendship. They shook hands on parting. The pressure of their hands was an unspoken commitment.

17

From then on Benjamin Lenz came every day to the office in the Potsdam barracks. How many rifles had Theodor issued to his *Bismarck-Bund*? Had preparations been made for Marinelli's escape? How often did the couriers travel between Leipzig and Munich?

Benjamin knew everything; more than one told him. For this reason he took Theodor to the others. Theodor expected that he would find faces known in Munich: Klatko, the pensioner from the battles over the Upper Silesian plebiscite, the deserter Conti from Trieste, the CSM Fritsche from Breslau, the former police sergeant Glawacki, the bookbinder Falbe from Schleswig-Holstein.

For a whole week he went to the meetings. He went to the smoky, ill-lighted dives, which smelt like beer cellars; he listened to the voices of the speakers, some of them high and shrill, others graveyard deep. He heard the applause of a thousand listeners, stood close beside them, smelt their sweat and their poverty, saw the flickering of their pupils, saw hard-bitten faces on scrawny necks; angular fists on thin, exhausted-looking wrists; moustaches untidily combed over toothless mouths; the black gaps of missing teeth between parted lips; bandages drenched in iodine over bare arms. He saw women with thin, straight-combed, water-pale hair, the poverty of those who were pregnant, their dry necks and their

thin, transparent, yellowish skin, hanging in folds. He saw
mothers with big-headed children at their flaccid breasts. He
saw youngsters with unruly hair falling over bold foreheads,
but marked already by toil and sickness, with eyes unnatu-
rally deep in their sockets. He saw young girls in shabby
shoes, their faces pale, their eyes searching for men, their lips
painted; and he heard their shrill, shameless voices. He saw
how they drank, could smell the schnaps, could not
understand their dialect, and smiled blankly when someone
bumped into him. These people were alien to him, their faces
were the faces of strangers, not from his world, not of this
world. He was not sorry for them, and though he saw that
they must suffer, he could not imagine what sort of suffering
was theirs. He might perhaps have understood an individual
case, but in this multitude there were no contours, no fixed
point. Everything swayed and swam. He could not tell the
manner of their loving, nor the fashion of their weeping. He
watched the way they ate the bread which was in their coat
pockets, how they pulled it out between thumb and forefin-
ger, at the same time pulling it to pieces and stuffing it into
their drooling mouths with the flat of their hand. But what
sort of tongues did they have, what sort of gums? What did
they taste? Sometimes, when they cheered, it was threatening,
and much the same sound as a cry of hatred.

He had no love for them. He was afraid of them, was
Theodor Lohse. He hated his own fear. Lieutenant Lohse,
said Benjamin Lenz, this is the German people, whom you
imagine you are serving. The officers in their mess are not the
people. And Benjamin Lenz was delighted. This was the way
of Europe, where one never spoke of what one did, and vice
versa. Where one thought of officers and students as being the
people. Europe, where nations exist which are not peoples.

And then Benjamin Lenz took himself to Trebitsch and told

him of Theodor Lohse's development and his treachery. He had long since betrayed what he had learnt through Theodor, had Benjamin Lenz. And he warned Trebitsch: a few days more and Theodor would betray arms caches, Marinelli's escape, the *Reichswehr*'s connections, the weapons of the *Bismarck-Bund*.

Benjamin Lenz was happy. That evening he folded banknotes into an envelope and mailed them to his brother.

18

How Benjamin Lenz loved these times and these people. How he grew among them, and prospered and gathered power, secrets, money, pleasure and hatred. His gloating eyes drank in the blood of Europe, his half-deaf ears seemed to hear the clash of weapons, the sharp crack of shots, the howling of the mighty, the last groans of the dying and the overwhelming silence of the dead.

Round about Benjamin the fruit spoiled on the tree and did not grow ripe, the ripe hated each other and corrupted the good, corrupted goodness itself, and dried up the sucklings' milk. Greybeards were trampled underfoot in the streets, women hawked their sick bodies, beggars brandished their infirmities, the rich flaunted their wealth, painted young men made their living on the streets, the seedy silhouettes of workers shuffled to work like corpses long buried but sentenced to drag on and on the curse of their earthly working days. Others drank, howled with insane jubilation in the streets, a last triumph before they disappeared, thieves put aside their furtive secrecy and displayed their loot openly, robbers forsook their hiding-places and carried out their trade in broad daylight; if anyone collapsed on the hard pavement, the man nearest to him would steal his coat. Illness galloped through the houses of the poor, across the dusty courtyards, hung about in the ill-lit rooms, broke through the skin. Money poured through the fingers of the well-fed, and theirs was the power; fear of the hungry nourished their worst instincts; the increase of their possessions inflated their pride; they drank champagne in palaces ablaze with lights; they clattered by car from business to pleasure, from pleasure to business; pedestrians died under their wheels, and the speed-crazy chauffeurs drove on; the undertakers went on strike, the metalworkers went on strike; in front of the brightly-lit windows of the food stores they craned exhausted necks, screwed up eyes which had sunk deep into their skulls, clenched feeble fists in torn pockets.

Self-important men spoke in Parliament, Ministers yielded to their civil servants and became their prisoners. Public prosecutors drilled with the storm troopers. Judges broke up public meetings. Wandering nationalist speakers hawked thunderous platitudes. Cunning Jews counted money, poor Jews were persecuted. Pastors preached murder, priests swung cudgels, Catholics became suspect, parties lost supporters. Foreign tongues were hated.

Foreigners were spied on, faithful dogs were put down, cab horses eaten. Officials sat behind their counters, protected by grilles, unapproachable, safe from fury, smiling and commanding. Teachers bullied out of hunger and anger. Newspapers invented horror stories about the enemy. Officers sharpened their sabres. Students fired shots. Policemen fired shots. Small boys fired shots. It was a nation of gunfire.

And Benjamin lived among distorted faces, twisted limbs, hunched backs, backs which had been flogged, clenched fists, smoking pistols, violated mothers, stranded beggars, drunken patriots, foaming beer mugs, clinking spurs, workers who had been fired on, bleeding corpses, desecrated graves, the mass graves of the murdered, exploded safes, iron clubs, trailing sabres, tinkling medals, generals on parade, and the gleam of helmets.

Oh, how Benjamin Lenz loved all this! How he must have hated, and how he must have fed and swelled that hatred! He looked upon the gruesome living and scented the stink of decay in advance. Benjamin waited. They would fall victims to him. They would tear one another to pieces and he would witness it. How Benjamin loved Theodor, the hated European, Theodor; the grim and cowardly, gross and cunning, ambitious and insatiable, greedy and frivolous, class-conscious, godless, overweening and servile, downtrodden and persistent Theodor Lohse! He was the young man of Europe: nationalistic and self-seeking, devoid of belief and of loyalty, bloodthirsty and blinkered. This was the new Europe.

19

On the night of October 20th, at eleven o'clock, Marinelli was freed. He sped to Berlin in a car which was ready and waiting, and went to Potsdam, where the driver had orders to deliver him to the barracks, to Theodor Lohse. Theodor was waiting for him. Marinelli was put into uniform the next morning and stayed in barracks. On October 21st Benjamin Lenz came and greeted Marinelli. He then took Theodor with him to the Russian, Rastschuk, who was employed in a bank.

Theodor was glad to have a talk with Rastschuk. They drank liqueurs. Rastschuk was so large and so powerful that he quite filled the little drinking shop. He spoke very quietly, but one heard him just the same. When he looked in the direction of the waiter, the waiter would turn round as if he had been called. Rastschuk was quite tremendous.

Benjamin Lenz told him about the springing of Marinelli, his flight and his presence in the barracks. This was very painful for Theodor, who grew hot under the collar because Benjamin was constantly interrupting his story by appealing to Theodor for confirmation of the accuracy of his words. 'Isn't that so, Herr Lohse?' he would ask, and Theodor would remain silent.

What, in fact, did he know of Rastschuk? That he had been a White Guard and was working for the overthrow of the Bolsheviks. So Lenz said. So said Rastschuk himself. But Theodor did not believe it. Anyway, it was too late for second thoughts. Theodor went with Benjamin Lenz. He was his ally.

Benjamin has drawn up a plan. Theodor Lohse will learn about the preparations for November 2nd. He will then report to the organisation. But Lohse lays down terms: what will he receive for this valuable information? After the success of November 2nd he must be given a leading and eminently visible position. Today, Theodor Lohse represents a danger. Two weeks divide him from November 2nd.

To give the others confidence, Lohse passes on secret orders.

Orders come for Theodor Lohse. Letters from friends in Munich, in which there are trivial phrases: Alfred is fetching Paul on the 2nd. This sentence means: the Berlin police are calling on the army for help. Or: Our old friend has engaged himself to marry Victoria. And that means: The Minister for the Army has come to an accord with the organisations. And: Martin is going to the children for a week. Which means that Marinelli has gone to the *Bismarck-Bund*, with greetings from Theodor and orders to prepare the young people in the university for November 2nd.

Lenz received these letters. He took them to Rastschuk.

In exchange Theodor learnt that the Saxon Order was being brought to Berlin, that nothing was planned for Potsdam, that a hundred and fifty-two Berlin police had gone over to the communist workers.

Theodor reports this to Seyfarth in Munich. He writes: 'I could give you a lot of fresh news, if we could meet. I've no patience for writing. I'm busy.'

So the student, Kamm, comes to Berlin.

'I'm sending young Kamm to you,' writes Seyfarth. 'Show him Berlin. It's his first visit.'

Theodor, Kamm and Benjamin Lenz went about Berlin. Kamm had money, and they spent it. They drank in the Tanzpalast and in the Kaiser-Wilhelm bar, and Theodor met his old friends there, and there was a big party. They left the cafés, the dives and the dance halls, and let themselves be picked up by whispering touts on street corners and led into gambling clubs. It was late, but in those smoke-filled rooms one noticed nothing, and one heard only the flutter of shuffled cards, laughter, the rustle of banknotes, the clink of a plate.

Theodor, Kamm and Benjamin sat in armchairs, away from the tables. Kamm had no more money. He looked to Benjamin for the price of his fare home.

He was only given enough to buy a third-class ticket on the express.

'One should be unostentatious!' said Lenz.

Then they began to go into details.

Lenz demanded 'real publicity' for Theodor Lohse after November 2nd. The whole national press must mention him by name. The saving of the city, of the Fatherland must be attributed to him. Otherwise, Theodor had the means to do very well for himself elsewhere.

'You could be killed before then – the pair of you!' said Kamm, polishing his nails with a piece of chamois leather.

'Just let them try,' said Lenz derisively.

He took from his pocket the mustering plans for the Saxon Order. Lenz and Theodor saw Kamm to the station.

Kamm stood in the window and waved.

'Say hello to Seyfarth!'

'Don't forget Paul!' said Kamm.

Lenz then left. He pushed his way through the hurrying crowd of office girls, bumping into painted women standing about looking lost. It was if the night had overlooked them.

And Benjamin Lenz went to Rastschuk. They hurriedly altered the mustering plans. Lenz had given Kamm the original.

'We must work honestly!' said Benjamin Lenz.

20

A few days before November 2nd, Dr Trebitsch vanished.

His uncle Arthur had arrived from New York. He owned an agency for ships' tickets. He said 'Well,' and thrust forward his lower lip. He carried his money in his pocket, lots of money, German money. For dollars he had a chequebook.

He was of Austrian origin and had fled abroad rather than face an army medical examination. That had been thirty years ago. Now he no longer had a hair on his head. He had sons and daughters. The sons had served in the American army. The sons were brave and had given back to the armed forces what their father had stolen from them by escaping from his army medical.

Trebitsch's uncle was a widower. It was his first return to Europe for twenty years. He was called Trewith.

He was startled by his nephew's beard. He laughed loudly and a great deal and slept every night with two girls at a time.

He asked Dr Trebitsch whether he would not like to come to America. Why should anyone want anything to do with Europe? It stank and was rotten. It was a corpse.

Dr Trebitsch said: 'Yes!' His uncle cabled New York. He went to the American Consul. He took his hands out of his pockets and in general behaved politely.

Trewith suddenly loved his nephew very dearly. He was moved to tears because this youngster, whom he had seen in his cradle, now sported a long, orange, flowing spade beard, like a rabbi.

That such a thing should happen!

His brother Adolf was dead. His sister-in-law was dead. Far and wide across all Europe there was only one blood relation to be found and he had a long beard! It was touching.

Uncle Trewith stayed on and waited for his nephew.

Dr Trebitsch wired Munich for money. He went to Major Pauli, then he cleaned out his safe.

Cheques came in every day. Trebitsch telephoned everyone who had subscribed to the Voluntary Service Organisation.

Efrussi, too, sent his contribution. An association of big entrepreneurs advanced a subscription for fear of November 2nd.

Trebitsch forgot no one.

He went into the board of the *Deutsche Zeitung*, which had taken up a collection for an injured member of the volunteers. Trebitsch took away the funds.

He forgot no one.

One day before his departure he had his beard shaved off. His smooth, boyish face surprised his uncle at his hotel. Uncle Trewith wept for joy.

Trebitsch then wrote one letter of farewell, to Paula from the Ministry of Defence.

'You will never see me again!' wrote Trebitsch.

Paula rushed after Trebitsch. The post had delivered his letter to her office. The house was shut up.

On her way she met a young man with the face of a child, who paid no attention to her, although she was wearing a striking, lemon-yellow hat. This annoyed Paula, but Dr Trebitsch was a greater cause for worry. So she went on her way and saw outside a car in which was seated an elderly American, smoking a cigar.

Theodor called twice. He found Trebitsch's place locked up. Theodor came the next day with Benjamin Lenz. Lenz brought a picklock and the door opened easily. It had not been bolted.

They found the cupboards open. The drawers were open. A chair had been knocked over. There were old clothes and soiled laundry.

They telephoned Major Pauli. He knew nothing. Only that Trebitsch had taken money.

They asked at the offices of the *Deutsche Zeitung*. No one knew a thing, except that Trebitsch had taken money.

Lenz sat on the sofa and thought things over.

'He's run for it, Lohse,' said Benjamin.

At nine in the morning the bridge fell into Hamburg harbour. Dr Trebitsch was aboard the *Deutschland*.

His uncle Trewith ran below once again, and spotted a girl among the onlookers; how lovely that she had come. She had promised to the day before. He gave her a smacking kiss. Everybody saw him.

Then he ran back. The bell was ringing.

He ran so fast that his smooth, strong cheeks shook.

He stood and waved a big handkerchief. Dr Trebitsch waved too.

21

Benjamin knew a lot of people: Pisk the journalist, Brandler the film producer, Neumann the statistician, Angelli the magician, Bertuch the travel writer.

Pisk, the newspaper man, was a worthy fellow. He wrote for Jewish papers. Social sketches, sketches of ancient and modern society. When some Princess died, he would write about it.

But he also wrote about Captain Ehrhardt. He wrote about Noske's development. He wrote about Ludendorff's past. He wrote stories about Hindenburg's days as a cadet. He wrote about Krupp. He wrote about Stinnes' sons and daughters.

He wrote about Theodor Lohse. Why should one not write about Theodor Lohse? 'He is the coming man!' said Benjamin Lenz.

One of Pisk's ears stuck out. He wore his wide-brimmed hat askew, so that the brim shaded this ear. He wore his hat in cafés, too, as he did not wish to be noticed because of his ear. In this way people could not say that his good looks were flawed. The worst they could say was that he did not know how to behave. And everyone said that anyway.

But when he sat down with Theodor Lohse in the drinking shop, he had taken off his hat. That suggested a devotion which was not afraid to make sacrifices.

And Benjamin comes to the conclusion that Pisk has in mind to write a great deal about Theodor.

The *Morgenzeitung* is running articles on 'Men of the Revolution'. And in the *Morgenzeitung* it states that it was Theodor Lohse who, on a night of destiny, saved the Reichstag from destruction by the Spartakists.

There is talk in the mess about this article in the Jewish paper. The 'young people' at the foot of the table ask Theodor to tell them the story.

No, Theodor Lohse dislikes talking about himself. He says: 'Not worth mentioning.'

And although even the colonel is looking at him, and there is a pause in the meal and the colonel's cheeks are not quivering, he will not talk.

'Some other time, when it's appropriate!' says Theodor Lohse.

Pisk has conveniently left his wallet at home.

'The bill!' calls Benjamin Lenz.

And when the waiter stands by the table, expectant and leaning slightly forward, Theodor has to pay. For he is in uniform.

Sometimes Pisk says: 'Let's take a taxi!' Pisk gives the driver the address. On the way he gets out and Theodor Lohse drives on.

Sometimes Pisk has other requirements. Benjamin Lenz also has his requirements.

Theodor has now taken over Trebitsch's duties. He only has to parade three times a week.

The colonel is aware that Theodor has business in Berlin. At irregular but frequent intervals, the name of Theodor Lohse appears in reports and articles.

In Jewish newspapers the revolution is not well thought of.

But Pisk loves the revolutionaries. He lives off them. For some days past he has been wearing a monocle, and in his wallet he carries a membership card of the Agricultural Students' League.

In this fashion he is protected against street fighting and attacks.

Benjamin Lenz, too, wears a monocle.

One can see that November 2nd is near.

22

Theodor spent the eve of November 2nd in a nightclub with his fellow-officers. They held an assortment of painted girls on their knees. It was the moment to take leave of life. That is what the officers said to the girls. The idea of an early death made all the girls nostalgic. The orchestra played the 'Wacht am Rhein'. One client remained seated. Two officers lifted him to his feet. He was fat and heavy and drunk. They held him on their shoulders, then they let him fall. He fell under the table and remained sitting there. He played with the champagne coolers.

The day dawned grey. It was raining, and Theodor waited at the station for his company, which had to take up its position in the city at eight o'clock. It was Sunday. The city looked drowsy. It was raining.

At nine some workers demonstrated on Unter den Linden. The nationalist youth groups were in Charlottenburg. Between the two lay streets, houses, police. And still the city waited for a clash.

At nine it was still raining. The workers went through the grey rain. They were as grey, as endless as the rain. They came out of the grey districts, as the rain fell from the grey clouds.

They were like the rains of autumn, endless, relentless, quiet. They spread melancholy. They came, these bakers with their bloodless faces, as if made from dough, without muscles or strength; the men from the lathes with their hard hands and their sloping shoulders; the glassblowers who were unlikely to see thirty out: costly, deadly, glistening glass-dust coated their lungs. Then came the broom makers with their deep-set eyes, the dust of the brooms and the hairs in the pores of their skin. There came the young girl workers, marked by toil, youthful in their stride but with worn faces. Carpenters came, smelling of wood and shavings from the plane. And the enormous furniture removal men, as large and overpowering as oak cupboards. The heavy-duty workers came from the breweries, stumping along like great tree trunks which have learnt to walk. The engravers came, the metallic dust scarcely visible in the lines of their faces; the newspaper compositors came, nightworkers who had not had a night's sleep for ten years or more; they had bloodshot eyes and pale cheeks and were out of place in the light of day. The pavers come, walking the streets which they themselves have laid, but nonetheless strangers to them, blinded by their brightness, their breadth, their lordliness. They are followed by engine-drivers and railwaymen. Through their subconscious the black trains still run, signals change colour, whistles blow, iron bells clang.

But towards them, with youthful faces and a song in their heart, march the students with bright caps and gold-embroidered banners, well-fed, smooth-cheeked, with clubs in their hands and pistols in their deep pockets. Their fathers are schoolmasters, their brothers judges and officers, their cousins police officers, their in-laws are manufacturers, their friends are Ministers. They hold the power, it is for them to strike the blow, and who shall punish them for it?

The marching workers sing the 'Internationale'. They sing

out of tune, these workers, for their throats are dry. They sing out of tune, but with a power which moves, a power which weeps, a power which sobs.

The young students sing differently. Resounding songs from practised throats, full and rounded songs of victory and blood, well-nourished songs without pause or distress. There is no sob in their throats, only jubilation, only jubilation. A shot rings out.

At this moment the police spring into the saddle, swords drawn and swinging, coming out of the sidestreets, with police on foot sealing off the streets behind them. Horses fall, riders lurch, the paving stones are torn up, exploring fingers dig between them, stones rain upon the breaking walls of police. Two powers are trying to come to grips, the mass of the powerful and the mass of the powerless, and the police cordons have been torn asunder while the hungry are forcing their way towards the well-fed. Above the frenzy of the people rises the singing of those who are pressing from behind. Now some are singing and some are bleeding, and sometimes a shot splits the frenzy of the songs, so that for a fraction of a second there is silence and one hears the falling of the autumn rain, and the drumming of it on roofs and windowpanes, and it is as if it were raining on a peaceful world preparing to sink into its winter sleep.

But then comes the lament of a motor horn, sounding like a wounded beast, and from far off comes the confused sound of the streetcars' bells, whistles shrill, trumpets cry like children. A dog who has been crushed howls like a human, becomes human in the hour of its miserable death, chains and bolts rattle from doors and again a shot rings out.

From the university comes Marinelli with fifty young people armed with carbines, to reinforce the students. The fire engines come. Their hoses send forth cold jets of water that falls with a painfully powerful hiss among the people. For a few moments the crowd scatters. Then it reassembles. Little groups form and develop. A shot strikes a hose. On the pavement lie firemen's helmets. The hose is torn. Police clatter up in lorries. The street paving rumbles. The windowpanes tremble. The police are at once dragged down, stamped on, bloodied, scattered and disarmed. Workmen smash carbines over their knees. Women are swinging sabres, pistols, rifles.

From the grey northern quarters more hordes come pouring, carrying household implements, pokers, spades, axes and shovels. High up above, a machine-gun stutters. Someone lets out a cry, and at once thousands have turned to flee. A thousand hands are raised, pointing nowhere. From every rooftop, guns are pointing. From every rooftop machine-guns stutter. Behind every projecting wall crouch green uniforms. Black muzzles are poking out of every window.

Someone shouts: 'Soldiers!'

The asphalt rings with the clatter of hobnailed boots. The houses are taken over and the windows have become embrasures. Riderless horses whinny in courtyards, commands ring out, weapons clink.

Theodor waits on the Alexanderplatz. His company waits. He presses himself against a closed *porte cochère*. His company crouches on the pavement. A mounted policeman informs him that the city hall and police headquarters are under attack. Theodor marches off.

It is going to be a hard fight. He will be killed. He feels like weeping. He marches at the head of his men. His ears are full of the even tread of his men. He is going to die now. He can still feel, from the night before, the delicious pressure of a woman's soft body.

A worker's commando is fighting round the city hall and police headquarters. Their leader is a man with flowing locks, with a club in his hand. Now he seizes a worker's rifle and takes aim. Theodor throws himself to the ground. He lands in a filthy puddle. Dirty water splashes up. He fires from this position, at random. His men are running forward. He can see nothing, only the bulk of the pavement, and above it the flatness of a square stone. An explosion startles him. Human bones spin through the air. The bloody stump of a leg falls from a height. Then a boot with a foot in it.

It is burning. One can smell the fire and see the cloud of smoke fighting against the rain, rising. Theodor jumps up. Runs. The Jewish quarter is burning. Pots and pans are hurtling from the windows of dirty houses. People are leaping, too. A Jewess is gasping beneath the weight of a soldier. She lies sideways across the pavement. An old woman hobbles across the street. Her haste is laughable. The strength of her crippled feet is all too feeble. Her face is the face of a fugitive and her movements are halting. Children crawl in the mud. They are wearing yellow shirts and there are bloodstains at the edges. The blood flows away with the rainwater, along with horse droppings, feathers and straw, all flowing down the thirsty drains in the gutters.

White-bearded men hurry with flying coat-tails. Someone grasps Theodor by the knees. Someone whining for mercy. Theodor kicks out with his foot. The whiner falls back into a stream of blood. Red flares up. Flames lick the windows. Smoke breaks out of falling rooftops. Men with iron bars cry: 'Kill the Jews!'

Everyone is killing and being killed. He sees a head in the mud. A dying face. Günther's face. Theodor stares at it and suddenly receives a hard blow on the head. Blood runs down his temples. Red wheels spin and he falls. He sees the workers' leader. His mane of hair. The flying club. Theodor draws his pistol. The man leaps sideways. He swings his stick.

Theodor sees his white face. He still has not cocked his pistol, and already it is flying from his painfully struck hand. The man comes nearer and he can see the whites of his eyes which are full of hatred. The man yells: 'You killed Günther!'

Theodor runs. Behind him he can sense the hot breath of his pursuer. At his shoulder he can smell his enemy's breath, behind him he can hear his enemy's hastening steps. On soundless feet runs Theodor. He runs through silent, burnt-out, murdered streets. He runs through an alien world, through a long dream. He hears shots, drumbeats, cries of pain. All sounds are muted in the layers of some insulating substance. Now comes a turning. Does safety lie over yonder? Double the speed, gallop faster on winged feet! Now he looks back and there is no pursuer behind him. He falls into a doorway. Before him lies a lost rifle. He picks it up and runs on. The dead still live! He hates the dead. He finds himself among soldiers. Now he recognises his own men. Cheerful greetings come to him. The butt of his rifle bumps against corpses. He smashes it against dead skulls. They burst. He stamps on the wounded with his heels, their faces, stomachs, their limply hanging hands. He takes his revenge on the dead, who will not die.

Evening falls. A damp darkness lurks in the streets. It is a victory for law and order.

23

It was a victory for law and order. Two ministers fell. They knew too much about the secret organisations. Two new ministers were appointed. They knew more. But they were friends. They belonged to the Democratic Party. So they seemed to be democratic. Yet they were honorary members of the *Bismarck-Bund*. And they were in touch with Munich. And they feared the workers.

'To take preventive measures' was the technical term for the ensuing policies. Spies, whom everyone knew, infiltrated secretariats and party headquarters. The police would announce a 'weeding out of secret nests'. Spies would leap on some harmless and insignificant speaker at a meeting, and the papers would state that some long-wanted Bolshevik spy had at last been caught, but that it was difficult to discover his true name. *Agents provocateurs* would arrange raids on working districts, loading two or three hundred men onto wide, rattling trucks. 'Aliens', which meant citizens from former German territories, were quartered on the aerodrome in barracks, guarded by police and sorted into trucks which took them to the frontiers. In these barracks lived thousands from all over the old Reich, with their children, wives, grandmothers. Dirt led to illness. Illness ensured a high death-rate. Before the trucks came, each day saw several deaths. Soft-spoken, drunken men went through the Jewish quarters, demanding money from all those who were about to emigrate. They were paid. The Jews who did not pay were thrown into prison as Bolshevik spies for examination by the police. This went on for a couple of months. Then the Jews, whose tickets for the passage had expired along with their American visas, would be returned to the frontier. The National Citizens' League was allowed to carry arms. Its members used them. German princes put on uniform and drove through the towns. Old generals shuffled about wearing decorations and spurs. Striking workmen who stood outside their factories were stabbed, shot and beaten up by the National Citizens' League. The newspapers would announce that the workmen had threatened passers-by and could only be dispersed by armed force. Wandering preachers drifted through the streets. They spoke of a national renewal. All the citizens in their businesses, all the importers, the factory owners, the civil servants talked about this national renewal. The socialist newspapers expected fresh attacks at any moment. The police arrived too late and took evidence.

It was a victory for law and order.

Benjamin Lenz proved how useful he could be. The journalist, Pisk, brought out a report on Theodor Lohse. Other newspapermen asked for interviews. They dragged up all Theodor Lohse's past achievements. They invented new ones. Theodor Lohse, overwhelmed by fame, lived surrounded by journalists. Rich Jewish establishments invited him. He even went to the Efrussis once. What a long time ago that had been! How much he had achieved! Now he stood in the Efrussis' house, with politicians, bankers, writers: a guest, just as they were. Now he could approach Frau Efrussi not only as an equal, but as a hero, in uniform, and as a famous man. But now her voice had a very distant sound. She no longer smiled. Her kindness had vanished, no warmth was in her: she nodded to Theodor, who could scarcely feel the tips of her cool fingers, and her expression was almost one of scorn, as if to say: Well, look at Theodor Lohse!

Theodor was able to forget about Frau Efrussi when he was talking to Fräulein von Schlieffen, who was living with her aunt in Potsdam, and who danced very well. Theodor was no dancer, nor a specially good seat on a horse. Fräulein von Schlieffen, however, rode every morning. And although every officer in the garrison was at her beck and call, she gave Theodor preference. She was twenty-six, an orphan, from a famous family, but penniless. Her father had ended his life as a modest Counsellor of Embassy in Sofia.

The daughter had been raised by nuns. Her aunt had always looked after her. Now the time had come to look about for a husband. In earlier times this would have been easy, but under the Republic, as one grew older, one was more likely to remain single. In these modern times money was more important than connections. Of what account was her name? No von Schlieffen could previously have married a bourgeois. Now it could be done. One was still blonde, those two tiny, premature lines at the temples were scarcely visible, one could still display fine white teeth. Yet those legs were already distinctly thicker and, on many nights, sleep was not to be found for the longing of one's heart and body for a man. There was none so unassuming as Theodor Lohse. No other man with such fame, success and ambition still retained such shyness with women. He was over thirty, at the best age for marriage. He had a future. A woman who wanted to move out and up could make good use of his ambition. Elsa von Schlieffen had reached the age when one thinks sensibly, and she came of a family which believed in careers.

'Why don't you marry?' asked Benjamin Lenz.

'Marry!' said Lenz, threateningly.

The time had come to take leave of the army. For all the people in Munich cared, one could spend a lifetime in the *Reichswehr* and end up as a staff officer. Trebitsch's post was already filled. It was time to look around. What use was a day's popularity? Fame was short-lived! Tomorrow brings a fresh story and the newspapers are ungrateful. People forget. One is forgotten.

Benjamin Lenz wants to sit at the fountainhead, he has no need for affable friends, he needs men in high places. Benjamin needs no small lieutenants. He wants his information at first hand; insight into an important state industry.

Theodor must marry. This simpleton of a Theodor, in the hands of an ambitious woman, will rise to the highest office. 'Exploit the way the wind is blowing!' said Benjamin.

Clearly, he could no longer be a soldier. How he had grown up. A year ago he could still have lost his life as an officer.

And what did a year ago matter now?

A miserable time, ham rolls and coffee with skin on it at the Efrussis, vegetables once a week and *The Elders of Zion*. The elders of Zion were not as they were described in that book. They were not striving for power in Europe. They understood. They had money. Money was the greatest power of all. But it was not easy to come by. Theodor's capital had not been growing for a long time, and Benjamin Lenz said: 'Sell out! Anyone who has no inside information on the stock exchange is fleeced. They're as bad as the gypsies!'

Benjamin liked to see Theodor without spare cash. Benjamin willingly lends his friends money, cash down. He is a noble fellow, is Benjamin Lenz. He is delighted when he can help Theodor.

Munich would gladly have left Theodor in the army. But he was no longer dependent on them, as in earlier days. He notified them that he was sick. He was a neurasthenic.

91

Neurasthenia is not susceptible of diagnosis, said Benjamin Lenz.

Theodor retired from the army. The mess laid on an intimate farewell party. He informed Munich of his resignation and requested further instructions.

To him it felt as if he had pushed aside the last obstacles.

24

A week later he became engaged to Fräulein von Schlieffen. Benjamin advanced money for presents, flowers and the reception.

Benjamin's resources seemed inexhaustible.

Fräulein von Schlieffen danced no more, nor was she seen out riding. Suddenly she lost all her sporting inclinations.

She stayed at home and sewed monograms onto blouses, bloomers, handkerchiefs.

Theodor came to Potsdam every evening.

The first snow fell. There was a fire in the grate.

Once, Theodor brought his sisters along.

They sat in silence, curtsied to the aunt, and went.

They were bemused by the sound of the name: Schlieffen.

Theodor's mother never dared ask after his fiancée.

At home, it was a long time since Theodor had been the one who was put up with and looked down on. How good it had been of God to keep Theodor alive.

If only his sainted father were alive! thought his mother. She, too, was sewing monograms. With red silk she sewed rhyming proverbs of varying connotations.

The mighty Hilper was now Minister of the Interior. He knew Theodor. Did Theodor know him? His press secretary was that little reporter from the *Nationale Beobachter*.

They all liked Theodor. He was a likeable person, and modest despite all his achievements. He also had contacts. He seemed to get on well with the press, and he was well-connected socially.

Nothing was known to his discredit. He had never been entangled in litigation. His past was blameless. He was even trained in the law.

Why should Theodor not receive an appointment?

Hilper decided to find him a place. He even promised to do so.

Now Theodor went from office to office. Counsellors shook his hand, not knowing for what appointment he had been selected, though they knew the selection had been made.

At one moment the journalist, Pisk, brought his friend, Tannen. The name Tannen was a pseudonym. But Tannen was a chatty man, a smiling man, he smiled a professional smile such as jugglers do when they take their bows.

Tannen slipped little paragraphs into the newspapers. He reported that a new post had been created in the Secretariat for Public Safety, a sort of liaison post between the Ministry of the Interior, the Secretariat and the police.

The journalist, Pisk, went to the Minister and enquired.

'I've heard nothing about it!' said Hilper. For Hilper was a straightforward man, a headmaster from Westphalia and no diplomat.

'But it would be a brilliant idea all the same!' said Pisk.

And then Pisk mentioned that Professor Bruhns, the astronomer, was celebrating his sixtieth birthday.

'Has he distinguished himself?' asked the Minister, who was a classical philologist and knew nothing about astronomy.

'And how! He's one of the top meteorologists,' said Pisk, 'and he's published a two-volume work on Saturn.'

'Indeed!' said the Minister. 'Good of you to let me know. Should I write to congratulate him, or send a representative?'

'A representative, Your Excellency,' said Pisk.

Pisk did not give a damn about it, but he must find bridges, bridges towards the subject of Theodor Lohse.

'Did you know,' asked Pisk, who avoided categorical statements, 'that Lohse is to marry?'

'Ah!' said the Minister. 'Whom?'

'A von Schlieffen!'

'Schlieffen? Good name!'

'A good match, actually,' said Pisk.

'Rich?'

'Supposed to be well off.'

'*Donnerwetter*!' said the Minister, who had married a poor girl while he was still a professor.

'Smart youngster!' said Pisk.

'And modest!' added the Minister.

And then they talked some more about Professor Bruhns.

And Pisk wrote: 'The report about the new post in the Secretariat for Public Safety has been confirmed by responsible sources. During the past weeks a former officer has often been mentioned as the coming man.'

The wedding was in January.

25

For the first time, Benjamin Lenz went to a wedding. He did not so much go as glide in a car to the church door. For the first time he wore a morning coat and top hat, and later he sat at a table with officers and old ladies, and drank wine which he had paid for himself.

It was a splendid wedding. Theodor wore mess kit. Comrades similarly attired glittered, clinked and rattled. In Potsdam, people looked out of their windows and stood in front of the church, despite the cold.

The colonel made a speech, and Major Lubbe spoke, too, mentioning Count Zeppelin once, but only from force of habit and without particular relevance. Elsa made Theodor give a speech of thanks, so he had to stand up and hold forth, and the upraised eyes of his bride quite confused him. A great love for all those present flooded his heart, and a couple of times he stood up to shake the hand of Benjamin Lenz, who was seated opposite.

Benjamin was enjoying himself. This was the true European wedding. Beside him sat the widow of Major Strubbe, talking about Kattowitz, where she had lived her loveliest years. Benjamin was not listening. His profound gaze was fixed somewhere far away. He was thinking of Lodz, of his father's dirty barbershop. He could see the single, blinded mirror in the shop. How simple and how wise were the sayings of the old Jews in Lodz, how sharp was their wit, how measured their laughter, how good their food tasted, the food of the Jews, beaten, scorned, living in exile with no helmets and no means of shining or showing off. This was the true European marriage, of a man who had killed senselessly, worked without purpose and who would now beget sons who in their turn would become murderers, killers, Europeans, bloodthirsty and cowardly, warlike and nationalistic, bloody but churchgoing, believers in the European God who was worshipped through politics. Theodor will raise children, students with caps of many colours. They will fill schools and barracks. And Benjamin saw the Tribe of Lohse. There was work to do. They will murder one another.

And Benjamin listened to the telegrams as Major Lubbe read them out. Congratulations came from Pisk, from other journalists, from Hilper, the Minister, from counsellors and from Efrussi. Then Major Lubbe paused, breathing audibly, and read out a telegram from Ludendorff.

And every time someone spoke, they spoke paper words, European words. It seemed to Benjamin as if he had himself ordered this wedding, and that the Europeans were presenting him with a ridiculous slice of their lives, for his entertainment.

Entertained he was. By the parson who, with an air of resignation and as if he were letting something dreadful happen to him, kept pouring more and more wine into his glass and becoming more and more silent as his watery eyes sent heavenward their humble and beseeching looks. The colonel was noisy. He must have a weak bladder, for he was always pushing back his chair, disappearing, and returning after a few minutes with a fresh joke, at which the officers' laughter was short, sharp and indifferent. The eyes of old Frau Lohse, who sat on the colonel's right, slid here and there like small, shy animals. When the colonel spoke to her she smiled, and when he spoke to old Frau von Schlieffen Theodor's mother was thankful that she did not have to look at the colonel, but looked instead at her son, at Theodor and his bride. Frau von Schlieffen wore a stiff Potsdam coiffure, her hair was scraped back hard and showed her yellow ears which looked like old leaves, while the sight of her bun was painful to the beholder.

How Theodor joked; he kept telling his bride anecdotes, since he simply had to speak. And even if he said something trivial, Elsa laughed, because she simply had to be amused. He felt proud. His bride was beautiful, but now and again he thought of Frau Efrussi, and deep down, in his most secret depths, he debated the question: was she better and more beautiful than Elsa? This Jewess irritated him. Everything irritated him. Although he should in fact be delighted. He was taking a von Schlieffen to wife. On his account she was surrendering her titles of nobility, giving up that old, resounding name in favour of a name which was common-place, even if it was frequently mentioned and had conno-tations of fame. The first months were taken care of, a quiet home was rented. Benjamin, faithful Benjamin had exchanged the share certificates for currency. Today or tomorrow Theodor would enter his home. The day after that, and the days and weeks which followed, he would spend there. The days and weeks lay before him full of happiness; his nerves needed a rest. 'You must rest, my love,' said Elsa. He must rest.

In the front room he unpacked the presents. Outside the windows lay the night, the lamp shone redly in the bedroom. Elsa embraced him, hugged him, he caressed her, smelt her hair, stroked her neck.

Next morning, Benjamin Lenz sent flowers and a big picture. 'In memory of bygone days,' wrote Lenz.

It was a portrait of Theodor by the painter, Klaften. Elsa hung it in Theodor's study.

26

Benjamin Lenz had paid for it in dollars. Not too many dollars.

Theodor put up with his portrait. He was no longer afraid of it.

He wore a modern suit with padded shoulders and a single button on the jacket. He didn't feel at home in this outfit. He couldn't find the pockets, which were placed high and on the slant.

He forced his wide feet into narrow shoes made of thin leather. He froze, and his feet hurt, but he found them smart.

He should have gone to Munich. He had to talk with Seyfarth. 'Don't go,' said Elsa, 'they'll come to you.'

He was worried that they might not come. But he showed no trace of anxiety.

'My love,' said Elsa, 'I just have to admire you.'

And he allowed her to admire him.

He lost his way a little. He began to believe what she said, to believe what she believed.

She went to church. 'I'm used to it!' she said. And he went with her, because he was jealous.

She refused to enter a train compartment if there were Jews sitting there.

He would take her to another compartment.

They had to travel second class in the suburban railway. He bought no season tickets.

In Berlin she often felt tired. She wanted to take a taxi. And they took one.

She would look lovingly at Theodor's portrait. And Theodor realised that his anxiety at the time had been exaggerated. It had been the excitement. Yes, he liked the portrait. Klaften had painted it when he still thought Theodor was a fellow traveller, Comrade Trattner.

'When did he paint you?' asked Elsa. 'Do you know this Klaften?' And she was proud.

Theodor was waiting for his opportunity. He wanted to outline his career to his wife.

Once he did talk about it. He picked a suitable evening. The wind was blustering in the chimney. Elsa was sewing bright flowers onto a cushion. Theodor began to tell her about Trebitsch. He was a very dangerous Jew. Theodor had been the first to spot this. No one had listened to Theodor's warnings. Unluckily. Theodor did not mention the Prince.

But he did describe the painter, Klaften. And Thimme, the young communist. He allowed Thimme, the *agent provocateur*, to blossom. He made him out to be older, and a leader. And it had not been a question of the Victory Column. The whole of central Berlin was supposed to have been blown up. The explosives had been placed in the canals.

'Were you in mortal danger?' asked Elsa.

'Nothing to speak of,' said Theodor.

'Tell me about the farmworkers,' Elsa begged.

Theodor told. There had been no farmworkers. They had been vagrants, Bolshevik agitators, every one of them armed to the teeth. On that occasion Theodor had cleaned all the undesirable elements out of Pomerania.

'I really have to admire you,' said Elsa.

Theodor then told her about Viktoria, the bestial woman, the dangerous spy who had fallen in love with him and given the whole game away to him.

Elsa thought about this for a little and said: 'That's not actually very pretty!'

'My dear child,' said Theodor, 'people of our sort can hardly credit it!'

'And she was his own wife!' Elsa concluded.

'His very own wife!' Theodor repeated.

And they kissed each other.

27

Once every week, Theodor went to Hilper. His case was making progress.

Elsa had thought up a position for Theodor. It was to be called: Head of Security.

No such job existed. But the very sound of the title gave Theodor no rest. He kept thinking: Head of Security.

He was appointed, sworn in, congratulated. He assumed his duties. Ten police officers waited in the anteroom for instructions.

There were meetings. Between the police and the Secretary of State. Between the Secretary and the Minister. Between all of them. Theodor drove in a car.

The waiting policemen set to work. Since they had as yet nothing to do, they filled out questionnaires. They wrote down lists of communists who had been expelled, in triplicate.

Whenever Theodor came into the anteroom, they were bent over rustling papers.

Then work came their way. Theodor found his feet. He resumed his old activities. He sent out spies. And because the police were in any event carrying out arrests, Theodor had still more arrests made.

Lenz gave him tips. This was the address of the organiser, Rahel Lipschitz. Arrest her! The next day Stock, the pacifist, was to speak. Arrest him! The socialist students were holding international evenings. Speakers were to come from England. Arrest them at the railway station!

Theodor had arrests made. He himself conducted cross-examinations. Minor offences took on the aspect of high treason in his hands. He needed a press officer.

Pisk became press officer. He sent out horror stories to the press. Scattered among all sorts of articles on foreign affairs, he would slip in little notes of warning.

The press resounded with the dangers through which the Reich was steering. Underground agitators were at work. But the authorities were on guard. Details of arrests would end with the phrase: The cross-examination was continuing late last night.

The obstinate prisoners admitted nothing. The police struck them. A policeman would pull a man forward and twist his wrists backwards. This was a 'security measure'.

If the suspect answered Theodor's tricky questions, the policeman would reduce the pressure. If he would not answer, the pain was intensified. 'Answer,' Theodor would say.

All the prisoners would realise that there was a connection between their answers and the pain. And they would answer.

The prisons were bursting. The police were no longer arresting burglars. The magistrates let them go. If they did put a burglar in prison it was so that he could spy on the others.

The prisons filled up. Huts were built to take the overflow. It was a cold winter. The wind keened and blew clouds of dusty snow. The snow fell through the joints in the hut roofs, melted and froze again on the floor. The straw was damp — too damp to rustle — and smelt of wet earth. Through it crawled children with faces like parchment and ribs cracking together. The prisoners in the huts were forbidden to light candles, although the electric light bulbs were old and unserviceable, and the men sat together in the dark and sang. In faltering voices they sang songs of blood.

Sometimes Benjamin Lenz would go, with a permit from Theodor Lohse, to inspect. He took his soldiers with him. He handed out cigarettes to the men, and on little bits of paper he would give them advice and plans for escaping. Some of them did succeed in escaping from the huts. They came to Benjamin Lenz. For one or two of them he could arrange forged papers. But most of them had wives and children and were forced to wait for their transport. They waited for a long time. They were waiting for death.

Once Thimme came to Theodor. They swapped reminiscences of the old days with Klaften. The young man, Thimme, liked Theodor, and said so. 'I took to you at once!' said Thimme.

This man is dangerous! thought Theodor.

I must watch my step, thought Theodor. But he did not watch his step. After a few days he grew to like young Thimme. He was a gifted man, a sharp youngster. All he wanted was a job.

And it turned out that Thimme knew of hiding-places. The drinking shops in Moabit, in the cellars of which explosives and weapons had lain. Nowadays no more weapons were found there. But Thimme had the knack of finding them. He would uncover them the night before they were to be used. He knew ways in. He had keys. He was useful.

Theodor did not watch his step. Within the satisfying quiet of his house, within the fixed terms of reference of his post, which was a goal and yet not a final goal, a small peak leading to higher peaks, Theodor Lohse became easy-going, as he always had been until danger or a threat to his purpose made him watchful and sharpened his commonsense. Thus he became what Benjamin Lenz wanted him to be. He could no longer function without Benjamin. Theodor needed him in his work, just as he needed his wife at home.

28

At home he was aware of his own importance. Here, his word was law, and here what he merely dreamed came true. He was always served his favourite dishes, without having mentioned them. He found his clothes brushed, his trousers pressed, no buttons missing from his shirts. No papers went astray, his weapons were in their proper places – he loved weapons – and Elsa cleaned his pistol. She, too, loved firearms.

Nowhere was he so powerful as at home. If he was in a mood to be masterful, then he could indulge it. If he felt a longing for warmth, it was at hand. Nobody here doubted his wholeness. In the evening he would complain of tiredness. Elsa said: 'You're overworked.' He would talk about what he had accomplished. 'You have a sharp eye,' said Elsa, and he would consider himself a fine judge of men. 'I'm fond of Lenz,' said Theodor. 'He's a loyal friend,' answered Elsa. And he believed in Benjamin's loyalty. He loved to hear the song of the nut-brown maid: Elsa would play it, without being reminded, before they went to bed.

She liked neither the song nor Benjamin Lenz, nor did she believe in Theodor's wholeness. But it was necessary to give way in small matters, so as to have one's way in large ones. A von Schlieffen only married a commoner because she hoped that he would be able to achieve the highest government offices. This required, above all, eloquence. And she taught Theodor to speak.

He almost forgot his wife. He began quietly and then increased the power of his voice. He never spoke in his room. He spoke in their big salon. A thousand people listening attentively to him would strike him almost physically. He spoke well when he spoke with enthusiasm. His eyes glowed with a strange light. He believed his own words. His convictions came from his own speeches, grew with the ring of his voice and were confirmed by it.

He spoke of the need to save the Fatherland, and he won back the faith of his young people. All his experiences were erased. He honestly hated the enemy within, Jews, pacifists, plebs. He hated them as he had hated them in the old days before he had known the Prince and Trebitsch, Detective Klitsche and Major Seyfarth. Elsa, too, hated the enemy within. Elsa was patriotic. She talked about the nasty smell Jews had. And Theodor seemed to think that he remembered Trebitsch speaking Yiddish. Only about Benjamin Lenz did Theodor know nothing precise. Nor did he wish to. He numbered Benjamin Lenz among his friends, like the Jewish journalist, Pisk.

And always, after talking like this with his wife, his rage against the enemy within would mount next day and he would reach for his bloodthirsty work with renewed energy. These people who stood before him, under arrest, what were they in Germany for, anyway? If they disliked their condition, why did they stay? Why not emigrate? To France, Russia, Palestine? He put this question to them. Some said: 'Because Germany is my home.'

'Is that why you are a traitor?' asked Theodor.

'It's you who's the traitor,' they answered.

They were delighted to have a row with someone. And they paid at once for their insolent answer. The policemen at their side squeezed the bones in their wrists.

Sometimes men were brought before Theodor who had been beaten till they bled, red blood ran down their faces. Inside Theodor rose the old crimson flames, red Catherine wheels of fire spun before his eyes, jubilation sang within him, raised him on high, and he rejoiced, felt himself light and borne upwards as if on wings.

There was one man living whom he wanted to see: the man who had pursued him. Theodor could still see the man's flying hair, his white face alive with hatred, his arm raised high; he could hear the swish of the stick as it came down, feel the pain in the hand which it had struck. This man, who had seen Theodor as a coward, seen him, Theodor Lohse, as a coward on the run, was still alive. He sent his spies out in vain to find this man. They questioned everyone under arrest about his hiding-place. Every time a fresh arrest was made, Theodor hoped to come across the spoor of his enemy. It was pointless in most cases to torture these people. Either they knew nothing or they gave nothing away. Some gave false information, and when they were faced with their own lies, they would laugh. Or they would claim they had made a mistake. Hope could only come from one source, from Lenz. Lenz knew the man.

'In a manner of speaking, he is Günther's brother-in-law,' said Lenz, 'and this is a kind of vendetta. He wants to kill you, but I believe I am on his trail.'

Again and again it was a false scent. Every morning came Benjamin's call and fresh hopes. Every evening disappointing, painful news.

Lenz described him precisely. He was the brother of the girl whom Günther would have married, Lenz said. Sometimes Benjamin said: 'On account of whom Günther died.' And, when he forgot himself: 'On whose account you killed him.'

And this expression was disagreeable. Theodor would see the upper lip painfully drawn back, the white gums, the cross-eyed look.

But Lenz would also describe the man's dress and his habits. He had already almost laid hands on him. But one bolt-hole always remained open, through which the wanted man escaped.

'We'll find him,' Benjamin Lenz assured him.

But he did not find the man, Theodor's mortal enemy.

'There's something on your mind,' said Elsa, 'and you won't tell me.'

'My work,' said Theodor. And he began to talk about the political aims of the Fatherland.

29

The night refused him sleep, and its overwhelming stillness swelled Theodor's fear of the unknown, fearsome enemy. Was he out of the country? Was he living somewhere in Theodor's neighbourhood? Was he perhaps living in Theodor's building, disguised as a hall porter? Did not the waiter in the little coffee shop facing his office have the face of his enemy? The long hair, the pale expression of hatred. The powerful, ponderous tread. The broad shoulders.

Was that man living inside the uniform of the official driver who looked after Theodor's car? Might he not be lying in wait round any corner which Theodor turned? Might he not have placed a bomb in this house, under the bed?

Theodor put the light on, walked up and down the room a couple of times, looked through the window at the quiet night in the streets and the flickering lamplight and listened to footsteps in the far distance.

Later, as dawn was breaking, Theodor fell into a heavy slumber. Daylight brought fresh hope, fresh fear, and grim hours of waiting. This was the one thing which Theodor could not talk about at home. He would have had to tell everything, from the very beginning. About Günther, about Klitsche. That would have been no tale to tell, but a confession, a fall from the heights attained by such a struggle; self-exposure, suicide.

And that left Benjamin.

Benjamin listened, consoled, promised, gave the latest gossip, gave advice, found out what had transpired at secret conferences, learnt the secret plans of the government, photographed documents, sold them, brought others to Theodor.

He was a busy man.

The workers rose in the working districts, and the unemployed demonstrated, since they were no longer earning anything. The long and painfully restrained fury of the masses burst into flame again. Groups of the unemployed came in from Saxony, not by train but on foot, wandering along the broad State highways, through a wind awhirl with snow, forerunner of spring.

Indeed, spring came. It was already to be sensed on the streets, for the snow was melting and its edges were covered by a grey crust. But the hungry, the refugees, the escaped prisoners and the workers who, before their arrest, had already undertaken the flight from their homelands and had hoped to disappear without trace into the great city; the women, whose men had been killed, the Jewish emigrants from the east who dared not board a train – they felt the spring as a triple scourge. They had made friends with the stinging frosts of winter, with the crunch of snow and its soft flakes, but the bitter wind which carried with it the coming rains of April, which bit through their clothes and dried the pores of their skin, this was more than they could withstand.

They fell down in the streets, and fever shook them; with chattering teeth they awaited their last hour, and then lay rigid in the streets. In their pity, refugees, new arrivals, buried the corpses in the fields at night, when the peasants were not watching.

Spring strode over Germany like a smiling murderer. Those who survived the huts, escaped the round-ups, were not touched by the bullets of the National Citizens' League nor the clubs of the Nazis, those who were not struck down at home by hunger and those whom the spies had forgotten, died on the road, and clouds of crows cruised over their corpses.

Diseases lay hidden in the folds of the wanderers' clothing, their breath was diseased. The policeman who encountered them on their way inhaled the disease from their curses, and if they were not outnumbered and murdered they would die in a few days anyway. Soldiers perished in their garrisons. Patrols sent out onto the highways would creep along the side roads to avoid meeting the Great Sickness, and still would not escape death.

But in the cities they spoke of the national rebirth, and

Theodor gave lectures. Now, more than ever, they were threatened by the enemy within, and the neighbouring states on their frontiers were ready to march. High-school boys were drilling. Judges were drilling. Priests were swinging clubs. Before God's altars and in the beautiful great churches of the land, wandering preachers were holding forth.

Theodor was kept busy by all these high-school boys, students, leagues. He spoke in the evenings at public meetings and he spoke his way upwards. Already he counted for more than the Commissioner for Police, more than the Secretary of State for Public Security, more than the Minister.

He stood on the podium, and the ring of his own voice uplifted him. His wife sat in the front row. Entrances, doors, windows were guarded. Here he forgot every danger, even his enemy, the lurking one, the unknown. 'I really do admire you,' said Elsa, and she sat in the front row and gazed up at her husband, who had come far and was going farther. Head of Security – thought she – President of the Reich, Regent for the Kaiser to come. Dazzling celebrations in white halls, marble staircases, gleaming gold, full evening dress clinking spurs, music, music.

New elections had been called. Who knew if another, even more brilliant post might not be free.

The newspapers wrote: 'Theodor Lohse'. Reporters from foreign countries came. The 'great world' knew of Theodor Lohse. His photograph was in the big American papers.

'One of the top men,' they called Theodor Lohse.

Why not the top man?

30

Once Theodor went into his office late in the evening and found Benjamin Lenz with the safe doors open.

Lenz was photographing documents.

As he saw Theodor he drew his pistol.

'Quiet!' said Benjamin.

Theodor sat on the table, staggered.

'Quiet!' said Benjamin.

'Spy!' screamed Theodor.

'Spy?' asked Benjamin. 'You were with me on the other side of the fence. You betrayed mobilisation plans. I have witnesses. Who murdered Klitsche?'

'Let's go,' said Benjamin Lenz, and escorted Theodor to his car.

'And sleep well!' called Benjamin as the chauffeur pulled out.

And Theodor drove home.

His wife was still at the piano, before going to bed. The windows were open and mild March breezes were drifting through the curtains.

'You will have great tasks before you now!' said Elsa.

'Yes, my child.'

'We must be prepared!'

'I am prepared!' said Theodor, and thought about murdering Benjamin.

Benjamin Lenz went to his brother that night. It was a long time since the brothers had met.

'Here's money for you, and a passport,' said Benjamin. 'Get out today!'

And Lazarus, his brother, understood.

They did not know each other at all. Lazarus did not know what Benjamin did, nor how he came by the money and the passport, but he understood.

Lazarus understood everything. Someone would make a small, unimportant remark, but a whole world lay behind that small and trivial phrase.

One could say a single word to any Jew from Lodz, and he would understand.

Jews from the east needed no explanations.

Lazarus had soft brown eyes. His hair shone. He studied so hard that he made new discoveries.

'Can you interrupt your studies?'

'I must,' said Lazarus, and was instantly ready. He only had one bag. And the bag was packed. Almost as if he had expected this departure from one minute to the next.

'Are you a doctor yet?'

'For a year now.'

'What are you working on?'

'A gas.'

'Explosive?'

'Yes,' said Lazarus.

'For Europe,' said Benjamin.

And Lazarus laughed. Lazarus understood everything. What was Benjamin by comparison? A minor intriguer.

But this young brother, with his gentle eyes and their golden lights, could blow up half a world.

The Paris train left at twelve-thirty.

Benjamin stood on the platform.

'Perhaps I may follow you,' said Benjamin.

Then Benjamin waved. For the first time, he waved. And the train slid out of the station. The platform was deserted, and a man was sprinkling water from a green can.

Somewhere, many locomotives were whistling on the tracks.

Also by Joseph Roth and available from Granta Books
www.granta.com

THE RADETZKY MARCH

Translated and introduced by Michael Hofmann

Written through the stories of three generations of the Trotta family, *The Radetzky March* is a meditation on the Austro-Hungarian Empire and its eventual collapse. This is Joseph Roth's most famous and most acclaimed novel.

'Roth's masterpiece is one of the greatest novels written in the last century . . . magnificent . . . exhilarating, life-enhancing to read' Allan Massie, *Scotsman*

'He saw, he listened, he understood. *The Radetzky March* is a dark, disturbing novel of eccentric beauty . . . If you have yet to experience Roth, begin here, and then read everything' Eileen Battersby, *Irish Times*

'Over recent years, the poet Michael Hofmann's glittering translations of Joseph Roth have single-handedly given a vanished voice fresh resonance in the English-speaking world. Now Hofmann has surpassed himself with the jewel in Roth's crown. *The Radetzky March* is a majestically assured and engaging novel' Boyd Tonkin, *Independent*

CONFESSION OF
A MURDERER
Told in One Night

Translated by Desmond I. Vesey

'I have killed and yet I consider myself to be a good man.'

So begins the tale of former Russian secret agent Golubchik, holding court after hours in a tiny Russian restaurant on Paris's left bank. As he recounts his tale to a rapt audience they find themselves drawn into his futile quest to claim the noble name of his father, his destructive love affair with a beautiful model and his hatred for his half-brother, the rightful Prince. *Confession of a Murderer* spans rural Russia, cosmopolitan St Petersburg and pre-First World War Paris and alternately fascinates and horrifies the reader with its wild story of collaboration, deception and murder in the days leading up to the Russian Revolution.

'Worthy to sit beside Conrad and Dostoevsky's excursions
into the twisted world of secret agents' *The Times*

TARABAS
A Guest on Earth

Translated by Winifred Katzin

Set in the early days of the Russian Revolution, *Tarabas* tells the story of Nicholas Tarabas, a young revolutionary ignominiously dispatched from St Petersburg to New York by his outraged family.

'Roth is a consistently magnificent writer of prose'
Guardian

'Read all his books, his stories, his observations and wonder at the intelligence, natural poetry and humanity of a gifted and candid master storyteller' *Irish Times*

'Roth's philosophical acuity is matched by his deep compassion for the frailty of the human condition'
Sunday Times

THE LEGEND OF THE HOLY DRINKER

Translated by Michael Hofmann

The Legend of the Holy Drinker was published in 1939, the year the author, Joseph Roth, died. Like Andreas, the hero of the story, Roth drank himself to death in Paris, but this is not an autobiographical confession. It is a secular miracle-tale, in which the vagrant Andreas, after living under bridges, has a series of lucky breaks that lift him briefly onto a different plane of existence. The novella is extraordinarily compressed, dry-eyed and witty, despite its melancholic subject-matter.

'*The Legend of the Holy Drinker* is an alcoholic fairy tale . . . a dreamy Parisian Catholic setting, destitution softened by fairy tale' *Times Literary Supplement*

'This is a little book of sublime simplicity . . . magically told' *Daily Express*

THE STRING OF PEARLS

Translated and introduced by Michael Hofmann

'The Shah of Persia decides to visit Vienna. Seeing a beautiful countess at a reception, he demands to sleep with her. How to avoid a diplomatic débâcle? Captain Taittinger, a young cavalry officer, finds the solution: his former lover, now a prostitute, looks very like the countess . . . There won't be a better book this year' *The Times*

'In brief, artless, glittering scenes that burnish images of Vienna and its loveless and unloving citizens the novel sketches the decline and decay of an empire . . . with such sparkling subtlety that you scarcely notice how lightly the story carries the freight of history' *Sunday Telegraph*

'This elegant, melancholy fable . . . is a wonderful portrait of Vienna in the last century and of a society at the brink of dissolution' *Mail on Sunday*

REBELLION

Translated and introduced by Michael Hofmann

Rebellion is the story of a Great War veteran, Andreas Pum, who lost a leg and gained a medal. He marries, plays a barrel-organ, and is happy. But when he is imprisoned after a fight, life seems unbearably altered. Then a chance encounter with an old comrade who has made his fortune brings Pum to a world where he has a transfiguring experience of justice . . .

'A great writer of German, and a great writer of English, have warmly conspired' James Wood, *Guardian*

'Brilliantly observed and icily concise . . . *Rebellion* makes one eager to take the translator's advice and read the rest of Roth's *oeuvre*' *Sunday Times*

'Roth's writing, in this fine translation by the poet Michael Hofmann, is unambiguous, direct, his story told with the simplicity of a fable, though suffused with period detail and a poignant awareness of mortality's steady step' *Scotland on Sunday*

RIGHT AND LEFT

Translated by Michael Hofmann

Set in Berlin in the 1920s, *Right and Left* charts the rivalry of the two sons of a wealthy banker, one of them an early convert to fascism. It is a brilliant evocation of Berlin before the rise of Nazism; a society on the brink of disintegration.

'Until now, Roth has been neglected outside the German-speaking world . . . In the poet Michael Hofmann he has found someone who can successfully translate his pellucid prose without losing any of its melancholy glow'
Literary Review

'Roth . . . can pack more into a few pages than lesser writers can do in a few hundred. But his lightness of touch has a deceptive historical weight'
Times Literary Supplement

THE EMPEROR'S TOMB

Translated by John Hoare

The Emperor's Tomb is a magically evocative, haunting elegy to the vanished world of the Austro-Hungarian Empire, and to the passing of time and the loss of youth and friends. Prophetic and regretful, intuitive and exact, it is the tale of one man's struggle to come to terms with the uncongenial society of post-First World War Vienna and the first intimations of Nazi barbarities.

'Joseph Roth is one of those rare and welcome talents whose concision and deceptive simplicity send the cogs of the imagination whizzing into overdrive' *Sunday Telegraph*

'Roth is able to contain moral universes within the tiniest of narrative spans, and to convey almost unbearable pity in the plainest terms' *Scotland on Sunday*

JOB
The Story of a Simple Man

'Many years ago there lived in Zuchnow, in Russia, a man named Mendel Singer. He was pious, God-fearing and ordinary, an entirely commonplace Jew . . . '

So Roth begins his novel about the loss of faith and the experience of suffering. His modern Job goes through his trials in the ghettos of Tsarist Russia and on the unforgiving streets of New York. Mendel Singer loses his family, falls terribly ill and is badly abused. He needs a miracle . . .

'One of the great European novelists of the century'
Sunday Times

'Reading him is like reading a prophet: provocative, discomforting, full of insight and foreboding' *Tribune*

COLLECTED
SHORTER FICTION
OF JOSEPH ROTH

Translated and introduced by Michael Hofmann

'Joseph Roth's literary reputation is undergoing a welcome revival in this country. This is largely thanks to his English translator Michael Hofmann. The seventeen stories testify to Roth's remarkable talent. It is hard to define the strange quality of Roth's genius . . . ordinary words are what his fiction is about – his stories are elegant, realist fables written in laconic prose. Every line is concretely realised and Roth is a mesmerising writer . . . this is fiction at its best – so real, it is magical. These stories are not overtly political. But they illustrate how in life the individual is invariably defeated: by the state, by fate, by a lover. The collection demonstrates Roth's versatility and his genius' *Literary Review*

'In German-speaking countries, Joseph Roth is counted among the great novelists of the twentieth century' *Times Literary Supplement*

'The poet Michael Hofmann has performed such an invaluable service that it's a shame that the minting of medals has gone out of fashion. He has rescued from oblivion the works of one of the greatest European writers of the twentieth century, Joseph Roth, who is finally beginning to gain the serious attention he deserves' *Evening Standard*